POP
GIRL

POP GIRL

TALLIA STORM

AND

LUCY COURTNEY

■SCHOLASTIC

Scholastic Children's Books
An imprint of Scholastic Ltd
Euston House, 24 Eversholt Street, London, NW1 1DB, UK
Registered office: Westfield Road, Southam, Warwickshire, CV47 0RA
SCHOLASTIC and associated logos are trademarks and/or
registered trademarks of Scholastic Inc.

First published in the UK by Scholastic Ltd, 2015

Text copyright © Tallia Storm, 2015

The right of Tallia Storm to be identified as the author of this work
has been asserted by her.

ISBN 978 1407 15938 6

Printed by CPI Group (UK) Ltd, Croydon, CR0 4YY
Papers used by Scholastic Children's Books are made
from wood grown in sustainable forests.

1 3 5 7 9 10 8 6 4 2

www.scholastic.co.uk

For my gran, Tessa.
Inspiring doesn't begin to cover it.

1

My name is Storm Hall.

First let's get all the "storm" jokes out of the way. I've heard them all and at seven thirty a.m. in the dreech (that means miserable, by the way) Glasgow weather, I'm not really in the mood! No, my sister is not called Lightning; no, my hair was not electrocuted by a freak thunderstorm and, no, I do not have a face like thunder! Standing in the rain outside the school gates is hardly a laughing matter.

Not that I'm here as punishment, you understand. It was my idea and I'm dragging my best friend, Belle, along for the ride.

Being on school premises before eight a.m. is against the rules here at Endrick School. You'd think they'd be glad to see us so keen – but no. Mrs McCulloch will self-destruct if she gets a whiff of us breaking the rules.

While I'm waiting, I pull on my headphones, flick to an Ivy Baxter tune and crank up the volume.

Bam, bam, bam, BA-dada, BA-dada. Much better.

Let me catch you up on all things Ivy, Ivy, Ivy. In short, she is the greatest performer of all time! Belle and I got to see her a few months ago. It was the moment I knew what I wanted more than anything in the world.

To sing.

Forget everything else. Music is my life.

Belle and I are both singers. That's the whole point of this morning's little adventure.

So right now, I'm leaning against a wall outside the gate trying to look cool as I read Belle's text. She's running late – no surprise there!

Belle is far better at covert operations than I am. She is Scottish, after all, and the best James Bond ever was Sean Connery, right? But then I'm Scottish too, and my spy skills are somewhat lacking!

I text her quickly:

Mission control intel reports all clear. Proceeding to Stage 1.

I turn up the collar on my jacket and give the front gate my best here-I-come look. (Already I'm thinking James Bond might fancy me as the new teen Q?)

I slide my phone into my pocket and press myself a little more closely against the wall. Correction: against the pinboard against the wall. The pinboard still has pins in it. "Heyyyy!" I yell. (It hurts like mad!)

"Nice to see you too." My BF has finally rolled up.

"Belle!" I hiss, rubbing the back of my shoulder. "Thought you were running late?"

Belle gives a nod. "We're not outside MI5 – relax!"

We head inside the building through the large front doors. The first part of the mission – sneaking in without being seen – is a success.

The corridor is quiet and dark with no sign of life. On a normal morning there are lights on and everyone is yelling. School is strange without people around.

We're passing the staffroom. I don't think any of the teachers are in yet, but just in case, I throw myself on my belly and wriggle past. It's harder than it looks on TV and it's not long before my elbows start hurting. Can you be a secret agent without mastering the commando-crawl?

Urgh, major knee-fluff alert. I don't think they swept the floor last night!

Belle is looking down at me, glaring. I give her a big grin as I get to my feet. Not far now. The corridor has never seemed so long in my life!

In front of me, Belle pushes open the door to the main hall. . .

In we go

Mission accomplished.

And now the hard work really starts.

This is our last practice before I go to Hawaii. After that term will be over. If we don't sing together today, it'll be too late.

OK, hold up. *Hawaii*? I hear you say.

I KNOW!!!

Not everyone gets a chance to fly off on once-in-a-lifetime holiday, let alone during term time. I mean, Hawaii! Six islands of flower-scented gorgeousness halfway round the world. Mum and Dad have been talking about going for so long – well, Mum's been droning on and Dad's mainly been listening – that I can practically hear the beach music already.

Oh, wait – I can hear the music because the last Ivy Baxter song I played was a Hawaiian-style track and it's totally stuck in my head. Earworm. That steel guitar! I can almost feel the splash of the bright water on my skin, smell the flowers and hear the rhythm of the sea on the shore...

I start hula dancing in the empty hall. Belle gives me a what-are-you-doing look. You may be sensing that I am easily excitable – well, I am.

"You know you love it," I say. "Hawaiian hulaaaaa, baby!"

For a second Belle holds my gaze. Is she jealous of the trip? Or thinking I've simply lost it? Just as I'm about to stop moving, Belle cracks the biggest smile and laughs.

"You're the worst spy, but ... those hips don't lie," she half sings, joining in.

This one I know and we sing a verse and the chorus.

Singing takes over. I'm completely comfortable with Belle so I speed up my dance moves, adrenaline whirling through my body. With a final rush of energy, I launch into a perfectly executed roundhouse kick. Haiiiiii-YA!!

"Oof!"

Ah. Oops.

I seem to have connected with a body. And that body is now lying on the ground making groaning noises.

2

"Oh my god, Storm. Did you just kill someone?" Belle says, her own crazy dance moves coming to a stop.

"Oh, wow!" I say, worriedly, as I reach down to haul the groaning boy back on to his feet. I'm too shocked to keep my voice down. "I'm so sorry, I didn't see you. Are you OK?"

"Sure. I get kicked in the back most days of the week." His voice sounds weak with shock.

My stomach swoops as I recognize him.

Great. I have managed to half kill Colin Park.

Tall and thin with brown hair that's always in his eyes, and trousers that are always a teensy bit too short, Colin Park was new at the start of term and is possibly the most annoying boy in the whole school. (This takes some doing – maybe I should be more impressed?)

Everywhere I go in this place, Colin pops up like a piece of burnt toast. We are in all the same classes. He's always on my bus. And I don't want to sound big-headed, but I'm sure he only joined the school choir because of me.

I've been doing my best to ignore him all term, and now I've managed to kick him to the kerb. Literally.

"Storm thinks she's a ninja. It's a medical condition, you know. Excuse us," says Belle, sliding up beside us as I do my best to brush Colin down. I have left a massive boot print on the back of his jumper.

"I'm really sorry, Colin," I say.

Belle yanks me to one side. "Don't you *dare* be nice to him. You'll only encourage more stalkery nonsense. He'll follow you around even more than he already does," she hisses.

"I just practically *killed* him. And he's got a crush,

he's not a stalker," I hiss back.

I turn and pat Colin gingerly between the shoulder blades, as he leans, his hands on his knees, and coughs. "You know I can hear you both, right?" he says as he straightens up.

Belle winds her arm around Colin's shoulders and pulls him close. He looks a little surprised.

"Between you and me, Colin," she says very quietly, "you aren't supposed to be in the building."

"I'm not?" he asks.

Belle sighs like she has the weight of the world on her shoulders. "Storm and I *should* report you," she tells him. "Health and safety procedures and all that."

Colin looks alarmed. "But you're not going to. Are you?"

"What do you think, Storm?" Belle asks me.

I am having difficulty keeping a straight face. The thought of getting into trouble is clearly freaking Colin out. He looks from Belle to me and back again.

"I think that if Colin could do us a *teensy* favour," I say after a long and agonizing moment, "we could forget the whole rule-breaking thing."

"Of course. You name it," he says at once.

"Keep watch for us?" I say, before Belle gets carried away and says something outrageous. "If a teacher comes, knock twice on the door. Like this."

And I demonstrate on the little window set into the double doors.

"Got it," says Colin. "And thanks."

"That was inspired, Storm," says Belle as I close the hall doors gently behind us. She glances back at the window where Colin is giving us the thumbs-up.

I don't reply. I am staring at the beautiful, empty stage.

"All mine," I say in bliss.

"And mine," Belle objects as I leap up the steps and grab the microphone. "I want a go too, you know, Storm. Storm?"

The microphone fits my hand perfectly. I press my lips to the cold mesh and close my eyes. I'm not in Endrick High School any more. I'm on the vast stage at the Hydro, gazing out at ten thousand fans.

They have been queuing for three days straight to get into the arena, and they are roaring my name. It sounds like a thousand thunderclaps. Storm! Storm! Storm!

"Thank you, everyone," I say dreamily, my eyes still closed. I imagine my voice booming around a stadium, a touch of feedback adding to the thrill. I am wearing my fiercest outfit. My skinny PVC jeans are practically tattooed on to my skin. My perfectly fitted, ripped white crop looks amazing under my gold sequinned Paul Frank bomber. Accompanied by some serious bling in the form of my TS knuckle dusters. I am ready.

A single spotlight picks me out of the darkness.

"It's great to be here. I have dreamed of this moment since I was a little girl. I'm so honoured to share it with you."

I lift my hands above my head and stamp the ground with my black Converse to count in my invisible backing band.

I had a feeling that this was the place to stay.

))

I had a feeling that everything was going
    my way.
I had a feeling my dreams were trying to
    say.
I'm not going home 'cause I am gonna
    stay right here.
California.
I'm not going home, 'cause in my heart it's
    so clear.

"Earth to Storm!" Belle shouts, snapping me back to reality. "I want a turn before Mrs McCulloch gets here."

I open my eyes.

I am almost surprised to see Belle looking up at me with arms folded and a frown on her face. Where did the banks of screaming fans and the twisting overhead lights disappear to? Talk about a comedown.

"Couldn't you wait for me to finish my song?" I say, back into the real world.

Belle taps the ground with her shoe.

"May I remind you," she says in acid tones, "that I didn't sneak into this place early this morning just to be your audience?"

"Come on, Belle, give me another minute. It's not like you want to make a career of this stuff like I do."

Belle glares. "Don't you ever think of anyone but yourself?"

"That's not fair," I protest. "I think about lots of other stuff! I think about music, and food, and clothes, and. . ."

"Me?" Belle enquires. "Do you ever think about me, Storm?"

"I'll be seven thousand miles away next wee—"

"Oh, poor you," says Belle, her voice dripping with sarcasm. "What about me? I'm risking a detention all over again. I want to sing *now*. It's almost ten past eight, Storm. We organized this break-in so we could *both* sing—"

The double doors at the back of the hall fly open with a bang.

Belle stops ranting in mid-stream and whirls

round. I am already preparing excuses: "The curtains were on fire" might work? I will kill Colin Park for definite next time. Whose idea was it to make him lookout anyway? Oh, yes. Mine.

Then I realize that it's not Mrs McCulloch at all. It's Emily and Gwen Douglas.

3

You'd think Emily and Gwen Douglas would be a less scary option than Mrs McCulloch our singing teacher, wouldn't you? They can't give out detentions. But, believe me – I would take detention over this, any day.

The twins wouldn't look out of place in a rugby scrum. Night-sky black hair dragged back into the tightest plaits you've ever seen, their arms and legs bulge with muscles and their blue eyes are like pools of icy water.

When they aren't thrashing kids on the hockey field, they're thrashing them in the classroom. They are two fear-seeking missiles always looking for a target.

Right now, that target is us. Oh good.

Colin hovers in the background as Emily and Gwen swagger into the hall. He seems to be mouthing, "Sorry!"

Belle gives him the kind of glare that can melt plastic. (Phew. Now at least I'm not the only one she's mad at.)

"Well, well, well," purrs Emily while Gwen slings her hockey stick over her shoulder in a menacing sort of way. "What are you doing in here, you naughty little weirdos?"

"Look, Storm," says Belle, in mock surprise. "It's Emily and Dinner Douglas."

"My sister's name is Gwen," says Emily.

Gwen growls. I'm not sure I've ever heard her speak.

I know what Belle is up to, but I'm not sure I want to go a round with these two. I stay quiet. (I know, a rare moment of silence from your wise-cracking heroine. Shocker.)

"That's what I said," Belle says coolly. "Dinner.

Dog's dinner."

Belle and I exchange a look; she is smiling.

"I tried to tell them they weren't allowed in," Colin pipes up.

"Shut up, Colin," snarls Emily. She switches her ice-blue gaze to me. "That was a nice little nursery rhyme you were singing up there. 'Baa, baa, black sheep', yeah?"

"And that, ladies and gentlemen, sums up Emily and Dinner's musical tastes," says Belle to the empty room.

"It's *Gwen*," Emily repeats. She is starting to get angry now. "You think you're all that, don't you, Pace? Everyone knows choir girls are freaks."

I'm getting brave from up on the stage.

"Sing with me, Emily?" I say, stepping forward, but still well out of their reach. "Just a couple of notes."

"Give it a go," Belle coaxes. "After us now. Tra la la..."

"La la LA!" I sing over the top of Belle's little tune in perfect harmony.

Emily reacts like we've just thrown something

unspeakable all over her sports top.

"Get away from me, freaks," she spits, lifting up her hands like she's warding us off. "I'm not singing anything."

"It must be awful, being tone deaf," Belle says to me, wiping away a pretend tear.

"Tragic," I agree.

We shake our heads and sigh. Gwen growls a little louder and starts patting the palm of her hand with her stick.

OK. My courage from the safety of the stage is fading fast.

"Guys," says Colin helplessly, throwing himself between the twins and the stage. "This is stupid. None of us should be in here right now. Don't you think you should save the arguments for somewhere a bit, er, safer?"

"Shut it, Colin," says Emily. "This is between us and the trilling pixies."

"Who's a pixie?" says Belle.

"I'm a pixie," I reply at once.

We start throwing the word back and forth

between us like a ball. "Pixie, pixie, pixie, pixie." It's completely hilarious, and it's not long before we're breathless with laughter. Essentially, I would call this the ultimate comeback technique – BOOM! I love it when we do this. We're so in tune. (Get it? Singing pun.)

Emily and Gwen look more perplexed than angry.

"You are so *weird*," breathes Emily at last. "Seriously, what is wrong with you?"

"Pixie," Belle snorts.

"You are in so much trouble," says Emily, her eyes gleaming with nasty delight.

When in doubt, brazen it out. Right?

"Oh, we have permission," I lie in my boldest voice. "We're setting up for choir. What's your excuse?"

Emily glances over her shoulder at the double doors, suddenly nervous. Belle is smiling innocently, looking unfazed by my lie. It's as if our argument never happened. Friends for ever stick together and all that.

I do feel bad for Colin though; he's sitting with

his head in his hands at the side of the hall. He looks like he might cry.

Faces are starting to peer in through the double doors. I realize with a flash of discomfort that the choir is gathering for morning rehearsal. We really ought to get out of here before Mrs McCulloch shows up.

But Emily isn't finished yet.

"I know all about you sneaking out of school before the holidays," she hisses. "I wonder how the school governors would feel about that? I don't suppose parents as stupid as yours realize how important education is."

I can feel what little confidence I had left beginning to slip.

"Don't you dare," I say furiously.

Emily gives her best shark's smile at my reaction. She can smell weakness like a fart in a lift.

"Then again," she says, "you're not exactly top of the class yourself, are you, choir girl?"

I hate Emily Douglas. I hate her more than I hate broccoli, more than I hate stupid jokes about my name. Just because she's clever *and* sporty, she thinks she's queen of the heap. I may not be the brightest, but that doesn't give her the right to talk to me like that.

"Shut up," I mutter.

It's hardly the retort of the century. I'm losing the edge in this conversation and I'm struggling to get it back.

Belle still has it though and, like a knight wearing a blue blazer and ponytail, she swoops in.

"Your pet gorilla isn't much better," Belle says, nodding at Gwen.

Gwen drops her stick with a clatter and I can't hold back a gasp. I do *not* want to see my best friend get pummelled by Grunting Gorilla Gwen.

Emily swells up like an angry balloon. Her voice is tight with rage. "*What* did you call my sister?"

"I called her a gorilla," Belle repeats cheerfully. "Lovely animal, lives in the zoo."

"Why, you—"

The Douglas twins launch themselves at Belle

and suddenly there's a squawking tangle of limbs and hair rolling about the floor. I'm frozen in place on the stage, looking on helplessly. It's not a pretty sight.

Colin groans and buries his head a little deeper.

A horribly familiar voice booms through the hall: "ENOUGH!"

4

Mrs McCulloch storms into the hall, her killer heels clicking like machine-gun fire. Behind her the rest of the choir is giggling, gasping and pointing.

"What on *earth* is going on?" she demands, coming to a halt with her hands firmly planted on her hips.

Belle is tangled somewhere between the twins. They break apart, all panting like dogs, but not before Belle gets a wallop on the shin from one of Gwen's hockey boots. Emily's shirt appears to be missing several buttons, much to Belle's very evident satisfaction.

"Well?" Mrs McCulloch demands, glaring at each of us. She must be the only teacher in the whole school who scares Emily Douglas.

"We ... we heard noises, Mrs McCulloch," the hockey horror mumbles, rubbing her scalp where Belle had been hanging on to one of her plaits. "We know the rule about not being in here without a teacher. We saw these two acting suspiciously so we came in."

"Acting suspiciously?" Mrs McCulloch repeats, raising her sharply plucked eyebrows so high that they almost disappear into her perfect hair. "Emily, this is not a tacky TV police drama. None of you should have been in this room, full stop."

Emily narrows her eyes at me. I make an impulse decision. LIE.

"You said Belle and I could be in here, Miss," I blurt out. "To set up the chairs."

Now all I need is for Belle to back me up.

"You did, Miss," Belle says.

Phew.

Mrs McCulloch fixes us with her piercing green

eyes. I don't know how she can look directly at both of us at the same time, but she manages it somehow.

"Emily? Gwen?" the choir teacher raps suddenly, making the twins jump. "Why are you still here?"

"Like I said, Miss," Emily bleats, "we saw Belle and Storm acting suspiciously—"

"So you thought you'd hang around and tell me all about it," Mrs McCulloch finishes, looking unimpressed.

Emily squirms. "It wasn't like that, Miss," she says feebly.

"Well, you've done your civic duty," Mrs McCulloch says. "So unless you are planning to join the alto section, I suggest that you leave."

Emily goes green. This does nothing to improve her looks.

"No way," she mutters, grabbing her sister's arm and backing towards the doors. "Come on, Gwen. Let's leave these losers to it."

The double doors slam shut behind them. The entire choir mutters their dislike. The Douglas twins aren't popular. No one likes being called a loser.

"Belle? Storm?" says Mrs McCulloch, striding briskly across the room to the piano. "You know perfectly well that I didn't give you permission to be in here without me. At this time of day, this is my room, and that is my stage, and that is most definitely my microphone. Clear?"

She looks at me as she says this.

I wince. How does she know that's what we came in early for? I swear our choir teacher has eyes everywhere.

"So, is there anything you would like to say in your defence before I string you both upside down from the gym bars?" Mrs McCulloch enquires as she settles down on the piano stool.

I exchange a panicked glance with Belle. We don't answer that, right? Or do we?

"It was my fault," says Colin.

Belle and I blink at this unexpected turn of events.

Mrs McCulloch folds her arms. "I'm listening, Colin," she says.

Oh my gosh. What is he going to say? Aarrgh!

Colin stares straight ahead through the tangled strands of his long brown fringe. "I arrived early, Miss, and came into the hall. This is only my first term at Endrick and I didn't know I shouldn't be in here. Belle and Storm came in to tell me that I was supposed to wait outside. Then Emily and Gwen arrived. You know the rest."

I don't know how I feel about Colin's so-called confession. I should probably feel grateful, but I just feel . . . annoyed. Guilty, maybe. (I hate owing people. Especially annoying people.)

"Hmm," says our choir teacher. "Well, as this is your first offence, Colin, I will let it go this time."

She studies me and Belle as she says this. We keep our faces perfectly straight.

"Take your seats everyone, please," she says with a sigh. "We have a lot to get through in the next thirty minutes."

I feel Belle sag with relief beside me.

I avoid Colin's eye as we head across the room to sit with the rest of the sopranos. But his gaze is like a magnet, and it's not long before I look across to find him watching me.

He's such a stalker.

"Thank you," I mouth.

He smiles. His teeth are nice; I'd never looked that closely before. Or was it that he's not smiled at me like that before?

As Mrs McCulloch bangs out an exercise for us to sing, I let my eyes drift across the rest of the boys. Colin's teeth are an exception, it would seem. Snaggle teeth are everywhere in the tenor and bass sections. So are tufty chins and red zits, greasy hair and bad glasses. What is it with boys who join choirs? Where are all the cool, good-looking, charismatic boys who love to sing? They must be out there somewhere. I just wish I knew where.

"Again," commands Mrs McCulloch as we warble our way up and down. "Tuning, tenors!"

We sound OK, I guess. I even feel a flash of pride on the high notes. The boys may be not much to look at, but choir is still my favourite part of the day because I can sing and no one thinks I'm weird for doing it. Scales don't go down so well in chemistry, unless I'm using them to measure out iodine crystals.

"Lovely," says Mrs McCulloch in approval. "Now 'Make Me a Channel of Your Peace'."

Mrs McCulloch wasn't actually telling us to make *her* a channel of anything. It's the piece we've been practising all term. The words are very deep and meaningful and nothing to do with TV channels at all.

There is a burst of chatter as everyone rushes to the piano to get the least dog-eared copy of the song. Belle fetches copies for both of us as I keep our seats.

"I love this piece," she says as Mrs McCulloch plays the intro. "The harmonies are so gorgeous, aren't they?"

I smile to keep Belle happy. I've never told her, but Mrs McCulloch's harmonies are dull. They could be SO much more if she let us improvise. Just a little. There's this chord towards the end that would be PERFECT for that special Storm touch: a crunchy, unexpected twist. Every time we sing it, I want to belt out the notes that could change it from boresome to *awesome*.

> Make me a channel of your peace,
> where there is hatred let me bring your love,
> where there is injury, your pardon, Lord,
> and where there's doubt true faith in you.

"I-in youuuu," I croon under my breath.

As Mrs McCulloch directs a sharp glance in my direction, I do my best to get to the end of the verse without any more runaway improvs.

Then there's a key change so cheesy you could call it a Wotsit. (Why? Why?? So predictable.)

Someone needs to come along and shake this thing UP. Someone like me, for instance.

Mrs McCulloch plays the instrumental middle section very neatly and correctly before we all plough on with the last verse. I zone out and imagine all the alternative harmonies and rhythms

I would use instead. No one would resist the tricks that I have in mind.

If this was *my* choir, I would attach a rocket to it and send it into the sky in a blaze of funky fireworks. Everyone would want to join. It would be the coolest club ever. They'd be queuing down the corridor at audition time. It would be as if Endrick High School was hosting *The X Factor*. For the first time in musical history, this choir would be *in*.

"... this choir would be IN."

There is a collective gasp around me and my mind jumps back into the choir room.

Oh. I didn't just say that out loud.

Did I?

5

No one is looking at me. I think I'm safe. Mrs McCulloch is just standing there with a grin on her face, looking at us all like we just achieved something massive.

Um. OK. What did I just miss?

I try getting Belle's attention, but she's not sitting next to me any more. She's too busy jumping up and down with her arms around Jade Miller. Everybody seems to be going nuts. Feeling increasingly bewildered, I look around the room for someone else to explain.

When I catch Colin's eye, he gives me a blinding smile and – not cool – a massive thumbs-up.

"Awesome, right?" he shouts across at me.

"Um, yeah?" I say. I'm clearly supposed to know what's going on. *Belle, rescue me now!*

Belle clearly hears my thoughts because she plops back down to me and pulls me into a tight hug. "I can't believe we're in!" she says, and her eyes are shining as brightly as stars.

"'In' as in. . . 'In' what?" I say.

Belle rolls her eyes. "I *knew* you weren't listening. You had this zoned-out look of a cow chewing grass. We've been selected as a last-minute entry for the National Choir Finals!"

That explains the hysteria. Not quite sure what all this fuss is about!

Mrs McCulloch claps her hands for our attention. "I know it's great news," she says, beaming round at us, "but it also means a lot of extra work. The show will be going out live on Saturday in London."

There's an extra burble of excitement at this.

"Does that mean we're going to London, Miss?" says Jade.

"No, Jade," Mrs McCulloch says, a little dryly.

"We're magically throwing our voices seven hundred miles south. There's no need for us to leave Glasgow at all."

Jade looks puzzled.

"I think Mrs McCulloch is being sarcastic, Jade," says Belle, rolling her eyes.

"We'll take a coach first thing on Saturday morning," Mrs McCulloch says when the laughter has died down and Jade is a little less pink in the face. "The show is being recorded live on Saturday evening. We'll stay in London that night, then spend Sunday sightseeing – " this raises a cheer "– before returning to Glasgow bright and early on Monday morning. And I mean *bright* and early."

The word "live" gets my attention. My heart rate has just gone up to about a hundred beats a minute. I put up my hand.

"Live on what, Miss?" I ask.

"National radio," says Mrs McCulloch. "This is a real chance for us to put Endrick High School on the map. We'll be doing 'Make Me a Channel of Your Peace', of course – it's the piece we know the best.

But we'll need to make a tiny change. Instead of the first verse being for the whole choir, we will turn it into two solos: one girl and one boy. It's important to demonstrate that Endrick High School Choir has *range*."

Oh. My. Gosh.

Suddenly, the National Choir Finals aren't looking lame at all.

They are sounding the complete *opposite* of lame.

Live radio! National exposure! *A solo!*

This is it. My dream. My chance to lead the choir with a solo. I can practically hear my heart palpitations bouncing through my skin with excitement. An audience. A real audience! This is my chance.

"As we are so short on time, let's audition for the solos right away," says Mrs McCulloch. "Do we have any—"

My hand shoots up before the choir teacher has finished her sentence.

"I'll do it!"

Belle looks at me strangely. She also has her hand

in the air. It looks like we'll have to be rivals for this one. I'm not worried. I'm pretty sure our friendship can take it.

"The clue is in the word 'audition', Storm," says Mrs McCulloch. "You are very welcome to *try out* for the solo along with the others. Let's hear the boys first."

In the hubbub that follows, I realize that Belle is still looking at me with that odd expression in her eyes. Surely she knows this isn't personal?

"Belle," I say, "all's fair in love and war and radio shows. Are you angry because I'm trying out for the solo?"

"It's not that," says Belle. "It's—"

I wave my hand at her for silence. Daniel McCready's trying out first, and if I'm going to be singing with him I need to hear what his voice sounds like. He looks like he would make a reedy sound, but it's more like a foghorn.

"*Make me a channel of your peas,*" he sings. He's flat.

"We're not singing about small green vegetables,

Daniel," says Mrs McCulloch. "Diction is so important. Thank you. Next?"

Everyone laughs. Daniel blushes and sits down again.

"Storm," says Belle, tugging at my sleeve.

"I can't believe Sanjit's trying out," I say, my eyes glued to Sanjit Singh as he makes his way nervously to the piano. "I've never heard him say a single word, and now he wants to sing a solo on national radio? He has guts, I'll give him that."

Sanjit's voice is small and quiet, but quite sweet if you're into singing mice. Mrs McCulloch smiles kindly at him as he scuttles back to his place.

"Good effort, Sanjit," she says. "Anyone else?"

Colin Park stands up. "I'll give it a go," he says.

"Storm," says Belle more urgently.

"Typical that Colin's trying out," I say over her. "I wonder if he's any good?"

Colin opens his mouth.

"Brace yourself," I whisper to Belle, giggling.

"*Make me a channel of your peace,*" Colin sings in

a voice that's nicely pitched and perfectly in tune. *"Where there is hatred let me bring your love..."*

"Lovely, Colin," says Mrs McCulloch. A few people clap.

"Wow," I say in surprise as Colin takes his seat. "He wasn't bad."

It strikes me for the first time that maybe Colin Park comes to choir because he likes singing and is really good at it. Maybe it's nothing to do with following me around at all.

Another couple of boys try out, but they are both hopeless. Tom Connolly just stands there with his mouth open like a goldfish. Mrs McCulloch has to give him a gentle push back to his seat because his legs basically stop working.

"Thank you, boys," says Mrs McCulloch when Tom has sat down. She checks her watch. "There's just enough time to audition the girls before registration. Who's going first?"

I'm already at the piano, smiling at the choir teacher. Belle is waving at me but I ignore her. I'm trying to focus.

"Storm," says Mrs McCulloch. "What a surprise."
I think she's being sarcastic. Again.

"Can I improvise, Miss?" I ask eagerly. "There are some flourishes that I've been dying to try out all term."

Mrs McCulloch sighs. "Something tells me I can't stop you. From the top."

As the choir teacher plays the familiar opening chords, I clasp my hands together and close my eyes. At last, I have an audience. In my imagination, it's not twenty-four bored-looking choir kids, but a whole auditorium. There are microphones everywhere. A gentle spotlight bathes me in a warm and starry glow. The nation holds its breath as I hit the first note.

"Make me a channel, oooh, a channel of your peace," I sing. "Where there is hatred let me bring your lo-o-ooo-OO-ve, where there is inju-u-ry your pardon, Lo-o-oord, and where there's doubt, oh, where there's doubt, the truest faith in you..."

There is silence as I sing. But I'm so wrapped up in the alternate melody I've chosen that I hardly notice.

"Oh, Master, grant that I may never, never seek, whoa no, so much to be consoled as to conso-o-OOO-ole, to be understood as to u-u-understand, to be, oh, so truly, truly loved as to love with all my so-ou-oul. . ."

The way this is going, I can even forgive the key change in Mrs McCulloch's piano part. I might even say that it sounds brilliant for once, because of all the stuff I'm doing over the top.

"Make me, whoa, make me a channel, a channel of your pea-ea-ea-EACE."

Everyone claps, including Colin. I feel like I'm floating on my own personal cloud as I drift back to my chair. I loved every second of that.

"Very impressive, Storm," says Mrs McCulloch. She looks a little flabbergasted. "Who wants to go next?"

Jade Miller has a go. She sounds too much like an opera singer for my liking, all warbly and loud. She's also sharp. I don't think she'll be much competition. Bonnie Lawrence does a loud burp in the middle of her solo by mistake, which makes everyone scream with laughter. Bonnie turns bright red, bursts into tears and rushes out of the room.

"Good luck," I whisper, squeezing my best friend's arm as Belle smoothes down her skirt and prepares to get to her feet. The double doors at the end of the hall are still going *thwacka-thwacka-thwacka* from Bonnie's hurried exit. "You'll smash it."

Belle looks like she wants to say something but changes her mind at the last minute. She gives me a half-smile instead, then walks over to take up her position at the piano. Mrs McCulloch launches into the intro for the eighth time today. She will be playing it in her sleep tonight, I bet.

Belle has a gorgeous voice that's as pure as a bell. She sings the solo beautifully, straight as an arrow and exactly as written. Mrs McCulloch beams at her and everyone claps – me most of all.

"You were amazing," I say proudly as she sits down. "I knew you would be."

Belle looks relieved. "Was I? I thought I went a bit sharp in the middle."

"You were perfect," I assure her. "Mrs McCulloch would be mad not to choose you."

My best friend just sung her heart out. I'm nervous and proud all at once. (This is playing havoc with my stomach – I feel like I'm going to throw up.)

"Thanks to everyone for trying out," Mrs McCulloch says. "It takes courage to stand up in front of your peers and sing. Courage that you'll need when you sing on national radio . . . Colin and Storm!"

"YESSS!" I roar, punching the air.

I knew that audition was a winner. Watch out, World, a Storm is coming! Bellowing YES was probably not the most courteous of acceptance speeches but, boy, did I nail it.

The boys have clustered around Colin and are patting him on the back. I have a terrible urge to run across the hall and hug him because we are going to be a team on NATIONAL RADIO.

I don't because that would be weird.

The bell rings out, shrill and demanding.

"Storm, come down off the ceiling," says Belle, trying to stop me from dancing around the hall as everyone else stacks the chairs against the walls. "Storm!"

"This is where it starts, Belle!" I squeal. "The dream. The life! I wish we could both have won, but—"

Belle stamps her foot and screams. She actually *screams*.

"*STORM!* Will you LISTEN to me for once in your life?"

I stop dancing. "Whoa," I say in shock. "There's no need to yell like that. You almost burst my eardrum."

"Are you listening?" Belle demands.

"What kind of question is that?" I protest. "Of course I'm listening! I always listen!"

Belle rolls her eyes. "Oh my gosh, Storm, you totally don't. But that doesn't matter. What matters is this." She looks deep into my eyes. "You can't do the solo."

I was afraid this might happen.

"Belle," I say in my calmest voice, "please don't let any jealousy ruin our friendship. I'd really appreciate it if you could just be happy for me."

"You can't do the solo," she says a little more loudly, *because you will be in Hawaii.*

7

I gape at my best friend.

"Hawa-what?" I say.

"Hawaii," Belle repeats. "The fiftieth state of the United States of America. The perfect paradise, seven thousand miles away. The place you are flying to tomorrow. The place you are returning from *after* the National Choir Finals. Hawaii."

I think I'm still gaping. My mind won't, CAN'T take it in.

"Hey, Storm, well done," says Colin, popping up at Belle's elbow. "I loved the improvisation you had going there. It's going to be great, singing at the Finals, isn't it?"

"This isn't a good time, Colin," says Belle. Her eyes are trained on me like searchlights. "Do you understand what I'm saying, Storm? Are you OK?"

I don't know what I am. I can hardly feel my legs.

"I'll fly back," I say at last, when I can get my voice to work.

Belle is silent.

. . .

"We'll change the flights."

. . .

"I can fly back in time for the Finals."

. . .

"I could do it on Skype."

Both Belle and Colin are watching me in silence.

. . .

"Or FaceTime."

. . .

"Or Mrs McCulloch could ring up my hotel and I could sing down the phone."

I know I am grasping at straws.

"I can still do it. I CAN."

Belle is shaking her head and all of a sudden, I'm

47

furious and I hate Hawaii. Of all the weeks. Of all the opportunities.

"I . . . I won't go!" I say.

As soon as I say it, I know that not going is a complete impossibility. My family have talked about nothing else for MONTHS. I can really see my folks being totally fine with me suddenly turning round and saying, "Actually, do you mind if I stay here? I'll feed the cat. Oh, and sing on national radio."

My dreams of stardom are falling apart before my eyes.

This can't be happening.

"Oh good, Colin and Storm, you're still here," says Mrs McCulloch, coming over to us. "We'll need to schedule some extra practice time for you this week to get your solos absolutely right. There will be some extra material where you'll be singing with the choir – I'll be writing the parts tonight. Can you meet me in the music rooms Monday lunchtime?"

"There's a problem, Mrs McCulloch," says Belle.

"There's no problem," I say quickly. There *must* be a way round this. "It's fine, Mrs McCulloch."

Belle is speaking over me. Rude.

"Mrs McCulloch, Storm has just realized that she'll be away for the National Choir Finals."

Mrs McCulloch's face drops. "Really? Where are you going?"

"Nowhere," I bleat.

"Hawaii," says Belle at the same time.

Mrs McCulloch pulls a face.

"Ah, of course. I've seen the notice on the staffroom board about your family trip. What an adventure!" She frowns. "It's a shame you didn't think of that before auditioning, Storm."

Thinking about that microphone without me behind it makes me feel physically ill. Seeing my face, Belle rubs my back sympathetically.

"That's a shame," says Colin.

He's so helpful. NOT.

"I'm sorry that you can't do the solo, Storm," says the choir teacher. "Truly I am."

My silent scream of despair echoes around the hall, pelts back towards us and smacks into Mrs McCulloch from behind. I imagine her rubbing the small of her back and wondering why it hurts.

"I wish things could be different. But what can I do?"

Change the Finals! I want to shout.

Obviously no one's going to change something national just because the Hall family has decided to take a once-in-a-lifetime holiday to Hawaii, are they? This is the *real* world.

"This was my big chance . . . and now I'm going to miss it!" I wail. OK. Enough. I have to get a grip or I will burst into tears and that will be VERY embarrassing for ALL of us.

I will be grown up about this. I will show strength of character and magnanimity. I remind myself how lucky I am to be going to Hawaii at all. I think of sun and sand and palm trees and boys in wetsuits. (Yes. Magnanimity is an excellent word to mark the maturity of this moment.)

"I suppose you'll have to drop my solo," I say, with a heroic gulp.

Mrs McCullough looks like I just caught her

eating a whole packet of biscuits. "We can't do that," she says gently. "I was wondering if perhaps Belle would do it instead."

Belle flushes in delight. "Really, Miss? Me?"

"You passed your audition with flying colours. I think you and Colin would be a very good match."

My stomach descends to my feet. All my magnanimity and maturity fly out of the window like a bad-tempered kite.

"You're giving my solo to *Belle*?" I demand.

Belle looks awkward. "Mrs McCulloch." She smiles. "Thank you."

What is Belle *doing*? She knows that I breathe first to sing, and then to live. Friends don't steal your *breath*.

"Good," says Mrs McCulloch briskly. "Decision made. Next time, Storm. Now hurry along or you'll be late for registration."

Mrs McCulloch leaves the hall with a *clickety-clack* of her high heels.

That's it. My chance has gone and my so-called

best friend has stolen my life. I'm so upset I can hardly speak.

"We'd better go," says Belle into the silence.

"I'm OK. I'll follow in a minute," I say. My voice feels raspy and weird, like it doesn't belong to me at all.

Belle recoils like I've slapped her. "Storm, I haven't taken anything from you. You're going on holiday!"

My best friend is perfectly sane and correct. But that doesn't help how I'm feeling. I start running – I *have* to get out of here before I say something awful. My hands connect with the double doors – *thwacka-thwacka-thwacka* like an out-take from *Grey's Anatomy* – I'm sprinting down the corridor like I have wolves on my heels.

All I want right now is to get as far away from Belle as I can.

"Hey, Storm! Wait!" Colin Park is following me.

I speed up.

"Storm!"

My lungs give out as I reach the cold air outside.

I lean against the wall with both hands, my head down, fighting the tears and gasping for breath.

"Storm," says Colin anxiously. He's a bit out of puff but not as bad as me. "Are you OK?"

I shake my head hard and concentrate on breathing.

"You really were good," Colin continues. He puts a hand cautiously on my shoulder. "Miles better than everyone else. I'm sure there'll be other chances for you, with a voice like that. You'll be famous before you know it and the National Choir Finals will mean nothing. You'll be on something much bigger."

I wipe my nose with the back of my hand. It's not very ladylike, but I'm not in a ladylike zone right now.

"I want to sing so much," I say miserably.

"You will," says Colin. "And you'll be brilliant."

He sounds so certain that, for a moment, I wonder if he's got some kind of window into my future. The idea cheers me up a little.

"Thanks for coming after me," I say after a

moment. I offer a watery smile. It's an effort. After all, he's got a solo and I haven't. He's kind of hard to look at right now.

"No problem," he says. "Are you coming in?"

I sigh. "I suppose I'll have to."

If I go back in, I'll have to face Belle again. Maybe I should just bunk off for the rest of the day. That way, I can avoid her until after I get back from Hawaii. After she's sung *my* song. I grit my teeth.

"Meet me after school?" Colin asks.

"OK," I agree, without really thinking.

Wait. Did I just say I'd meet Colin Park after school?

He holds open the doors for me. As I walk slowly back into the warmth of the Endrick High School corridor with Colin beside me, it strikes me that, yes, I have just agreed to something that feels suspiciously like a date. Damn!

8

The first lesson is English. I sit as far away from Belle as possible. Unfortunately, this means sitting next to Colin, because it's the only spare desk.

"Are you going out with *him*?" Jade Miller asks, twisting round to goggle at me when Colin gets up to fetch some paper from Mr Ligeti's desk.

"I am sitting *next* to Colin Park," I correct with a sigh, using his full name. "It's not exactly the same thing, Jade."

Jade's eyes are wide. "You ARE going out with *Colin Park*!"

"They're made for each other," Belle says from the other side of the room.

Just the sound of my ex-best friend's voice makes me tremble with rage. A *real* friend would have understood my random act of emotion. Maybe even refused to sing my song. OK, probably not. Belle and I have been friends since for ever, which makes all this even worse. It feels like someone just pulled the ground from under my feet and tipped me on to my—

"Paper?" says Colin, giving me a sheet.

I don't know what we're supposed to be doing because I haven't been listening. I do my best to concentrate on what Mr Ligeti is saying about the highwayman poem.

"Atmosphere!" Mr Ligeti whispers through his beard so it ripples like a wind in the hedge. "This is all about creating a mood."

"Storm doesn't need any help with that," I hear Belle say.

I am itching to respond but I won't give her the satisfaction.

"Now, I want you to go through the poem and find the words and phrases that make the most impact on you. Away you go!"

The poem is big and romantic but really sad too, all about a highwayman who loves an innkeeper's daughter. It doesn't end well and is basically about betrayal. *Torrent of darkness*, I write with gritted teeth. *Blood. Shattered. Death.*

"I like the highwayman's outfit," says Colin.

The highwayman's outfit is all lace and velvet and thigh-high boots. It's definitely the best thing about the poem. (Although I'm not sure what this says about Colin's dress sense. Seriously? I guess the thigh-boots would fix his trouser problem. Ha!)

"You should totally get an outfit like that," I say. "Especially the lace at the throat."

"I had enough of that at Scottish dancing lessons," says Colin.

Jade smirks knowingly at me when I laugh, and makes kissy shapes with her lips. I stop laughing at once and send her a look to curdle milk. The last thing I need is for Jade Miller to put it about that Colin is my boyfriend.

Belle leaves the lesson before I do, which is a

relief. We aren't in the same maths class and she does German while I do French, so we don't actually see each other until lunch.

I end up sitting with Colin. Again. Belle sits at our usual table with our other friends.

My stomach tightens as I catch the drift of their conversation.

"Great news about the solo, Belle."

"Yeah, really awesome!"

"I can't believe you'll be on the radio."

"You'll be famous."

Bonnie Lawrence turns her head and stares at me. I swear I can see pity in her eyes. All of a sudden my mac-and-cheese tastes like dust and I can't wait to get out of there. I snatch up my tray and walk silently past.

Belle stands up. "You're behaving like a little kid, Storm."

I slam my tray into a slot on the trolley with considerable force, then spin round to face her. Belle gets right up close to me, her nose almost pressing against my own.

"I'm not going to apologize for this," she says. "And even if I did feel guilty about it, after the way you've behaved today I'm not going to feel guilty any more."

Inside, I'm screaming for words to come out. I don't make a sound. Instead I can feel tears rising and all of my concentration goes to fighting them back. Be calm, I tell myself.

Then Belle explodes so loudly that the rest of the canteen falls silent and gapes at us both.

"*You* are so selfish! Oh, I feel so sorry for you – you're going to Hawaii instead of singing a solo. It's SO COMPLETELY TRAGIC!"

I step back, startled.

Belle hasn't finished. "How hard can it be to say 'Well done, Belle'? I've done something really good here and I'm *proud* of it. You on the other hand are a horrible person. I can't believe we were ever friends."

"I—"

"Mrs McCulloch offered it to me because YOU CAN'T DO IT!" Belle roars.

There is a scattering of applause from the canteen. My cheeks feel scarlet with humiliation. Belle has never shouted at me before. I truly don't know what to do.

"Come on, Colin," I say stiffly. I stalk out of the canteen with Belle's fury still ringing in my ears.

"Newsflash, Storm!" she shouts after my back. "The entire world doesn't revolve around YOU!"

Colin is still with me as I hurry outside to the playground with my hands pressed to my hot face. I can still see Belle's expression in my head. It makes me feel sick. I can't look at Colin because I don't know what I'll see in his face. He probably thinks I'm a horrible person too.

"Stop following me, Colin!" I snap. I know this is unfair but I'm so shaken up that I'm not thinking straight.

"You told me to come with you," he points out. He seems unruffled by all of this.

"Well, I'm now telling you to go away!"

I find the quietest, darkest corner of the school that I can, sink to the ground, curl my arms around my knees and tuck my head down between them. I stay like that for the whole of break.

I've never felt worse in my life.

I can't believe we were ever friends.

It's a very long afternoon. Belle is nowhere to be seen. Thanks to the canteen scene, people look at me and whisper and no one smiles at me.

When the bell finally rings for the end of school, I grab my bag and run down the corridor with my head down like a charging bull. Hawaii can't come quickly enough.

"Watch where you're going, choir girl."

I glance back as I reach the double doors to freedom. Emily and Gwen Douglas are propped up by their lockers, hockey sticks in hand. And standing beside them – is Belle.

I can't believe my eyes. My ex-best friend has not only turned her back on me, but appears to have taken up with my two worst enemies. Could today get any worse?

"Hi," says Colin as I fly through the doors and

take a big gulp of air.

"You again?" I groan.

"We said we'd meet after school," Colin says, keeping up despite my best efforts to out-walk him. "What time is your flight?"

"First thing tomorrow."

"Are you looking forward to it?"

"I'm looking forward to getting away from this place," I grimace.

"How are you feeling about Belle?"

What's with the questions? They make me think about stuff I don't want to think about. And something tells me that Jade Miller is going to pop up at any minute.

"I'm feeling fantastic, thanks for asking," I say. Heavy on the sarcasm.

Colin doesn't seem to notice. "You don't look fantastic," he says. "You look like you've seen a ghost."

I sink on to the bench inside the bus shelter. I've come out of school so early that no one else is here yet.

"I need a holiday," I mutter, rubbing my eyes.

"Lucky you're going to Hawaii then," Colin says. "Although I hear that the waves and the flowers and the Pacific Ocean are a very stressful environment."

I laugh reluctantly. "Oh, yeah?"

Colin grins. "Take it from me. I go to Hawaii on Google maps all the time."

My bus pulls up.

"Mind if I come along?" says Colin.

There isn't much I can say.

During the journey home I stare out of the window at the passing traffic, brood about my argument with Belle and hope that Colin will shortly spontaneously vaporize. The feeling of injustice is still strong. So is something else.

I think maybe it's shame.

"Is this your stop?" says Colin as I get off the bus at the bottom of Waverley Road.

"No," I say, walking away from the stop with him still hot on my heels. "I always get off the bus several stops before my actual stop because I like walking uphill for half an hour."

"That seems a bit extreme," he says.

"Colin," I say. "Has anyone ever told you about sarcasm?"

He smiles. "I'm being annoying, right?'

"Kind of."

"Wouldn't be the first time," he says. "My sister pretends she doesn't know me at school."

I am surprised. "You have a sister?"

Colin scratches his ear. "I'm not entirely sure," he says.

I laugh. Properly this time. For a weirdo with ill-fitting trousers, he's surprisingly funny and if I'm pushed to admit it (and I mean *really* pushed), he's actually kind of cute. I mean, if you like that sort of thing.

"Thanks for walking me back," I say when we reach my gate.

"Any time," he says.

He's standing uncomfortably close to me. So close that I can see the freckles scattered across his nose. AAAHH! I have a strange feeling that Colin

Park is about to kiss me. And an even stranger feeling that maybe I'd like him to.

What do I do now?

"Well, um, see you, Colin," I say, stepping away from him hurriedly.

Too hurriedly. My heel catches on the step and I tumble backwards. My bottom scrapes the brick edge of the flower bed and I land with one buttock on the path and one in a patch of prickly flowers.

It hurts.

I am more embarrassed right now than I have ever been in my life.

The front door flies open.

"I thought it was you, Storm," says my big sister, Tina. "Why have you planted yourself in the flower bed?"

"She wants to grow bottom roses," sniggers Jake, my little brother.

Behind him, Alex – my other brother – explodes with laughter. Jake and Alex are at the age where bottom jokes are the funniest thing ever. I flush bright red.

"Flower-bed-surfing?" says Dad, appearing, coffee in hand, as I scramble to my feet and hope the path will open up and swallow me whole. "I thought we'd save that for Hawaii."

"Bottom roses!" Alex screeches.

I turn to Colin.

"Bye, then," he says, making a hasty exit.

Several pairs of hands reach to drag me back to my feet and dust the earth off my skirt. Everyone is talking and laughing at once. I look hopelessly round at Colin, to see that he's already melted away down the road.

"Ooh," says Mum, appearing with a handful of knickers dangling from one hand. "Was that your boyfriend?"

"Why are you all so EMBARRASSING?" I

demand as I march into the house.

"We're not the ones who landed in a flower bed in front of our boyfriend," Tina points out.

"He's not my— Oh, what's the point?" I mutter. "I'm going upstairs."

I need to take my mind off everything. The National Choir Finals. Belle. And Colin.

I crawl under my bed and lie there for a while, staring at the slats above my head. I've always found it easier to think under here. I've done it since I was five years old, when I thought the dancing dust specks were fairies and I would talk to them about stuff.

Today has NOT been a good day. Have I lost my best friend? Have I encouraged a stalker? And why was Belle hanging out with Gwen and Emily? I try to breathe deeply. None of this matters for the next couple of weeks. Think about Hawaii.

Sun. Surf. Swishy palm trees . . . much better.

When I am feeling a bit calmer, I crawl out again. It's time to start packing.

"I don't think you'll need that, Storm," says Tina, plonking herself down on my bed and eating carrot sticks as I try to cram my faux-fur jacket into my suitcase. "Snow isn't forecast for Hawaii any time soon. Tees and bikinis. That's all I'm taking."

I eye Tina's massive suitcase out on the landing. "That's a LOT of tees and bikinis."

"Oh, and shoes." Tina offers me a carrot stick. "That's mainly shoes."

I read somewhere that Hawaii can get cold at night. I pick up the jacket again. Why is it miaowing? Suddenly the cat jumps out from inside. He scratches me and scarpers on to the landing.

"I don't think you need to pack the cat either," says Tina.

I'm too busy sneezing to answer. I can handle the cat as long as I'm not *handling* the cat, if you know what I mean. Having pets is not all it's cracked up to be.

Hawaii is all I can think about now. It makes me feel a tiny bit better about missing the National Choir Finals. And a tiny bit worse about Belle. Perhaps I did behave badly? I sit down on the bed and stare at my suitcase, wondering how she is.

"Bernie!" Mum yells from downstairs. "Did you just eat that tub of ice cream I left out? There was enough in there for the six of us to have for tea tonight!"

"Not me, Megs," Dad yells back.

Alex appears at the bedroom door. He looks sick. Well, that explains where the ice cream went.

Tina gives me the thumbs up and sidesteps out of the room before Alex has the chance to be ill near her. I sneeze three more times in a row.

Did I say this was going to be a holiday?

10

Storm Hall @stormhall_14

In the AAAIIIRRR. Hawaii here we come!

It's happening! I am actually on my way to Hawaii. I have a *Movie On* magazine in my hand. Glasgow feels like light years away already.

My phone vibrates in my pocket.

Colin Park @iamcolinpark

@stormhall_14 Hawaii has a species called the Happy Face Spider

OK. At least someone is paying attention.

Storm Hall @stormhall_14

Atlantic Ocean: big. Boring. Seen all the decent
films. #ha-why

Colin Park @iamcolinpark

@stormhall_14 It used to be illegal for girls to eat
bananas and coconuts in Hawaii #ha-because

OK. He's kind of funny. In small doses.

Storm Hall @stormhall_14

Hi New York! *runs between gates* Bye New
York! #shortbutsweet

Colin Park @iamcolinpark

@stormhall_14 Einstein's eyeballs are in a safe
deposit box in New York

Storm Hall @stormhall_14

A lot of USA is flat and yellow. #fact

Colin Park @iamcolinpark

@stormhall_14 Except for Appalachians and Rockies

Storm Hall @stormhall_14

Pacific Ocean: what I said about Atlantic Ocean only bigger. #howlong

Colin Park @iamcolinpark

@stormhall_14 75% of volcanoes on earth are in the Pacific

Jake and Alex have been having a punch-up in the row behind me for the last forty minutes. Dad's been in a twitchy sleep since Phoenix, muttering Hawaiian words now and again. Mum has been making lists and listening to meditation tapes for so long she's practically levitating out of her seat.

I've been doing all the DVT exercises Mum drilled into us, rotating my ankles and walking up and down the aisle, but I still feel like an old picnic table that's been left out over the winter. Thank goodness we only have an hour to go. I don't think I can cope with another in-flight meal.

What's more, Belle hasn't responded to any of my hilarious travel tweets while Colin has replied to *every single one*. I'm going to have follow him, aren't I? I have been obsessing about this since halfway across the Atlantic. A lifetime ago.

"Who calls themselves @iamcolinpark?" I demand, showing my sister Colin's tweets. "Talk about zero imagination."

Tina peels up her eye mask.

"Is this your boyfriend we're talking about? The cute one who walked you into the flower bed yesterday?"

"He's NOT my boyfriend," I repeat for what feels like the hundredth time. I file away the strange fact that my sister thinks Colin is cute.

She is crazier than I realized.

"I would never have a boyfriend with such a boring Twitter handle."

"What's the big deal? It does what it says on the tin," says Tina, settling her eye mask on again. "Yours

74

isn't exactly bursting with ingenuity, you know. And both of them are better than Bel Lemon."

"Who's Bel Lemon?"

"Your friend. @bellemon."

I snort with laughter. "I think you'll find that's Belle Mon. As in, Belle Monaghan Pace?"

Saying Belle's name gives me a stomach pain. I think of the last time I saw her, hanging out with Emily and Gwen.

What if she joins the hockey squad?

What if she turns into a sports freak?

What if she picks on me every single break time for the rest of my school life?

Tina turns and glares over the seat-back at our little brothers. "If you two don't stop hitting each other I will ask the stewards to strap you both to the wings of this plane. One on each side for balance."

The boys stop fighting and look anxiously out of the window.

"Hula!" shouts Dad in his sleep.

I only got the window seat because I pushed past Tina at JFK. The Pacific Ocean is like a vast, glittering sapphire. On and on as far as the eye can see. I am about to turn away from the window again when I spot an island on the horizon.

I grip Tina's arm, all irritation forgotten.

"Hawaii!" I gasp.

Tina forgets to be older and cooler than me and plasters herself to the window beside me, her nose squashed against the glass.

"Wow!" she squeals. "We're almost there!"

"We're there, we're there, we're there!" Jake chants in delight.

Hawaii creeps closer with every announcement from the captain about overhead lockers and foldaway tables. The excitement in the cabin is palpable now. Before long we're beginning our descent. When we touch down, the whole plane cheers.

"The air smells funny," Jake announces as we move through the terminal.

"A combination of frangipani and aeroplane fuel," Dad says, wheeling one of our three baggage-laden trolleys.

First impressions of Hawaii? There are a LOT of gorgeously tanned boys in the terminal, all wearing flip-flops and sunglasses and brightly coloured shorts.

"Please can I change, Mum? Please, please?" Tina begs, frantically applying mascara as we plough through the crowds.

"You can change at the hotel," says Mum in a brisk voice. "I'm dying for a cup of tea."

The queue for taxis is long but it doesn't matter. It's so lovely to be standing out in the warmth, breathing real air that hasn't been recycled a hundred times through a smelly cabin, feeling the breeze on my skin and gazing at the palm trees that line the road in front of us. We're here. It seems unbelievable.

"In the old days, it would have taken months to travel from Glasgow to Hawaii," says Dad. "And we've made it in twenty-four hours. Isn't that amazing?"

"Grab that taxi, Bernie," Mum says, ignoring him. "It's the only one big enough to fit us all in."

The taxi sweeps us round Honolulu in the blink of an eye. We are soon purring down a long, half-empty street listening to cheesy Hawaiian radio as the cabbie chats with Dad in the front.

Tina's got most of her make-up on by the time we have to stop for Jake to pee behind a roadside bush hung with amazing plate-sized flowers.

"So embarrassing," Mum mutters as the taxi starts up again.

After half an hour, we swing through a big set of gates, past a riot of flowers and into the Hokulani Beach Resort.

The hotel spreads before us, all wood, plate glass, traditional thatch and atmosphere. It is utterly beautiful in the calm afternoon sunshine. My travel-worn senses are dazzled by the sweet perfume in the air and the sound of the waves whooshing gently against the palm-fringed lagoon beach right outside the main building.

"I love it even more than I did online!" Mum squeals, clapping her hands as the cabbie helps Dad unload the taxi.

Mum is the kind of person who goes on StreetView to assess all angles of a holiday destination. She knows this place like the back of her hand already, and we haven't even made it through the main door.

"I can't get reception," complains Tina, squinting at her phone.

My sister is totally missing the point.

Who needs reception when you're in paradise?

11

Monday 9 a.m. (7 p.m. in Glasgow)

404 ERROR

THIS PAGE IS CURRENTLY UNAVAILABLE

Scrap what I said about reception.

Everyone needs reception.

I need reception – right now.

Twitter, Snapchat, Instagram, Facebook…the same message over and over. Unavailable. Unavailable. My online life is entirely unavailable.

"Don't you think I've tried that already, Storm?" Tina is painting her toenails the same vivid blue as the sea out of the window. "We get nothing around here. Nada. Zero. No Wi-Fi while their security is being fixed."

I wonder how I'm going to cope for an entire week without being plugged into any social channels. I'm going to miss SO MUCH.

The whole of Glasgow could get blown off the face of the earth on Tuesday, another band member could leave One Direction on Wednesday, Nori West could bring out her debut EP on Thursday and the first I'll hear of it will be when we're trying to touch down in a very-recently flooded airport next weekend.

I drop my phone irritably beside my bed.

Oh my gosh, the bed. It is incredible, it feels like drifting away on a massive marshmallow. Sleeping upright in economy is already feeling like a distant memory. Yesterday afternoon we were all SO tired, but after a decent night's sleep, the sea is twinkling temptingly at me through the window. I stroke the beautiful flower *lei* that was put around my neck by the hotel staff yesterday and think happily about my bikinis and all the Instagram snaps I'm going to—

Oh. Unavailable.

"When did Mum and Dad say to meet them and the boys for breakfast?" Tina asks, putting away her little blue bottle of Pacific-coloured varnish.

"Half past nine. What are you going to wear today?"

We spend a happy twenty minutes sorting out perfect Hawaii beach outfits. Tina goes for her electric pink Triangl swimsuit, complemented by her super-chic thigh-high gladiator sandals.

I opt for my favourite silk River Island maxi skirt with my white Public Desire platforms. My arms are bejewelled with an abundance of silver and gold bangles.

Once we've done our make-up, we head down in the big plushy lift to the even bigger, plushier reception area. There are chandeliers and huge rattan shutters and fans that spin quietly on the ceiling, ruffling the enormous potted ferns everywhere. People in white jackets nod and smile at us as we walk across the polished wooden floor.

I almost look over my shoulder to check who they are nodding at. This place is *swag*.

Tina marches into a huge banqueting room with floor-to-ceiling windows and a long white-clothed table groaning with some kind of state banquet.

"I don't think that's for us, Tina," I say, looking around for a smaller room with a cheese, ham, croissants and orange juice-type buffet.

But Tina's already waving at a table by the window and Mum, Dad, Jake and Alex are waving back. Jake has two pastries, one in each hand. Alex has his head practically inside a pineapple.

"Help yourselves!" says Mum, waving a slice of watermelon around like a conductor's baton.

"I was so overwhelmed when we came in that I only picked up a Danish pastry and a kiwi fruit," Dad confides. "But the coffee's good and I'm ready for seconds now. Come up and choose with me?"

I have pineapple, melon and rambutans (kind

of like lychees) to start with, followed by toast and chocolate spread and washed down with an enormous glass of fresh and zingy grapefruit juice.

I want SO badly to tweet about it all. A picture of my plate and a witty caption to make Belle laugh.

Not that she'd read it.

I swallow the sudden lump in my throat.

"Check out Shirt Family," Tina whispers, nudging me out of my funk.

Two tables along from us, a family of five – a big dad and four even bigger sons – are scoffing their breakfast in perfectly matching, full-on Hawaiian shirts, covered in coconut palms and parrots.

I do my best not to snort my grapefruit juice out through my nose. One Hawaiian shirt is bad enough, but *five*? A sensory explosion!

Mum puts down her empty teacup. "What are you going to do today, girls?"

"We're hitting the beach, Mum," Tina says. "We'll see you later."

*

To be honest, the beach kind of hits us.

Well, me.

I am so gobsmacked by the perfect curve of the lagoon, and the smooth shoreline, and the way the water starts transparent before *veeeery* slowly turning turquoise, and the cartoon-like perfection of the palm trees that I fall over my flip-flops and get a mouthful of Hawaii's famous white sand.

"I am *so* not with you," Tina mutters, yanking me back on to my feet and then speed-walking towards a lounger with its own straw umbrella down by the water's edge.

I sink down – on purpose this time – and run the glittering sand through my fingers. It's so pretty that I can almost forget what an idiot I just made of myself. The way it sparkles makes me think of ground diamonds. I think I could live in Hawaii for ever.

Tina has already attracted the attention of two volleyball-playing boys with nut-brown chests and perfect white teeth. With her blonde hair piled up just so on top of her head, her new electric pink

Triangl bikini, her spray tan and her best sunglasses, she knows how to work an audience. She'll have them buying her coconut cocktails within the hour.

I stretch out on the lounger for a nice lazy morning of magazine-reading.

It's so hard to concentrate though. Every time I settle into an article, Belle's face drifts into my head. Glaring at me, just the way she looked during our last conversation – if it could be called a conversation. (More a vicious attack, in my opinion.)

I've really messed up, haven't I? And I have no idea how to put things right. Being seven thousand miles away for an entire week without a phone connection is a problem. Anything could happen. Any*one* could happen. Like Emily and Gwen. And there's nothing I can do about it.

As I root around sadly in my beach bag for my headphones, I catch the insistent sound of drumming in the air.

A boy is sitting under one of the palm trees, playing a set of bongos. I sit up and squint through my sunglasses to see a little better. The bongos look home-made: big popcorn containers with lots of duct tape stretched across the top.

Boom, boom, dadada boom, boom, dadada. . .

Music always improves my mood. I find myself swaying gently to the beat. I would cut through the rhythms right there, I think, drumming along lightly on my thigh with my fingers and humming gently under my breath. I decide I don't need my headphones after all. I have a live performance right here on the beach.

Bongo Boy is building his rhythms now, layering them on top of each other like a big squishy cream cake. His long dark hair swings over his face as he plays. It makes me think of Colin Park and his over-long fringe.

I wish I was brave enough to go over and talk to him. Instead I lie back and soon I feel myself drifting off. The lounger is really comfortable, and the sound of the sea works like a lullaby. I must still be jet-lagged.

When I wake up Bongo Boy is still playing. I glance in his direction, and try to make my legs swing off the lounger and walk over to him.

No. Wait. What would I say?

How could I make him see that I'm not just a gawping teenager but someone who can truly feel the music that he's making? I would only make an even bigger fool of myself than I did face-planting into the sand during my grand entrance.

But I soon forget Bongo Boy. My sister is jumping around in the waves, squealing her head off like a mouse that's being repeatedly trodden on. I try to ignore her but—

"Storm! STOOORRRMMM!" she wails.

Oh my gosh.

Judging from the way she's hopping up and down on the sand she really IS in pain.

"What?" I gasp, rushing over.

"J . . . j . . . jellyfish," my sister weeps.

The beach ball boys are laughing now, kicking their ball around and showing no inclination to help. I glare at them and help Tina to limp out of the water. There's a big red lump on her shin. It looks really sore.

"You poor thing," I say, rubbing her back. "Do you want me to pee on it?"

Tina is so shocked that she stops crying at once. "No WAY," she says in disgust.

"It's meant to help the pain," I assure her.

"Oh my gosh, Storm, the answer is still absolutely and utterly NO! Are you insane? Just help me inside, will you?"

The hotel concierge is quick and efficient, fetching an ice pack straight away and making sympathetic noises. They reassure me that the sting isn't dangerous. Just, well, painful.

"Those boys were laughing at me," Tina moans as I help her shuffle into the lift with the ice pack tied around her shin.

"I don't think they saw," I lie. "They were just laughing at a joke."

"Yes," Tina says dolefully. "Me. I'm going to bed. This thing REALLY hurts. What a great way to start this holiday."

As Tina shuts the door, I realize that, basically, I'm on my own now.

I'm not sure I want to go back to the beach on my own, not with those stupid boys still there. I don't want to go to the gym or spa either. And there's no way on this earth I'm going to join my little brothers in the kids' club.

I can't go online. What am I going to do?

I head back down to the lobby, hoping that inspiration will strike.

And find Bongo Boy standing in reception, drumming his fingers on the desk.

It must be Fate.

12

Monday 2 p.m. (midnight in Glasgow)

I freeze.

Then I unfreeze again because I realize how stupid I must look with my mouth wide open. Bongo Boy obviously senses that someone else is in the lobby. He turns his head and looks at me.

"Hi," I blurt.

He smiles. "Hi, yourself."

He has a lovely musical voice. Just the way I knew it would be. He's quite tall and very skinny. His tan is a deep golden brown.

"You were on the beach just now," he says.

Edging a bit closer to him, I nod silently. Since my stunningly witty "Hi!", I seem to have lost my voice.

"Was that your sister you were with?"

I feel a little crunch of disappointment. Of course, he's talking to me because he fancies my sister.

"Cramp, was it?"

"Jellyfish sting. I said I'd pee on it."

He looks startled. I could totally kill myself right now. (*I'm talking about peeing to a guy I don't even know. How smooth am I?*)

"She didn't want me to," I add.

TOO MUCH INFORMATION, STORM.

"But you know, it'd help the pain. The pee I mean."

OH. NO. I NEED TO STOP TALKING. FAST. Why is my mouth not obeying my brain?? SHUT. UP!

Bongo Boy scratches his ear. "I'm Jeff," he says.

"Storm," I squeak. I'm deeply relieved at the change of subject. "And my sister's Tina. Well,

Valentina really, but only when she's in trouble."

"Your key, sir," says the receptionist, appearing like a white-coated mirage behind the desk.

Jeff pockets his key. "See you around, Storm."

"Yes," I say, staring as he saunters over to the lifts with his bongos under his arm. "See you."

So basically I just met the coolest guy ever and managed to say about thirty words of nothing, plus a bit about peeing on my sister.

The list of things I didn't ask about grows and grows in my head:

What music does he like?

Where is he from?

Why is he in Hawaii?

Is his family here too?

I didn't even ask about his bongos.

And was he flirting with me a tiny bit?

I replay our conversation in my head.

He'd said, "See you around, Storm," in this *voice*. . . I need to know what the voice meant.

BELLE! I REALLY, REALLY, REALLY NEED YOU RIGHT NOW!

93

If thought-waves work by volume, Belle will hear me for sure because I am SCREAMING inside my own skull. But as she's not even talking to me, she's hardly going to start thought-waving me back, is she?

I have to speak to her. I don't know what I'm going to say but I'll worry about that when she picks up. I go to press "call" on my phone before remembering. AAARRGH. No reception!! There are three clocks on the lobby wall showing the time in Hawaii, New York and London. I realize that it's about midnight in Glasgow. Belle wouldn't have appreciated a call from me at midnight even if we *were* still friends. "Police, Ambulance, Fire Service," she would have said in her most sarcastic voice. "What have you burned down now, Storm?"

I sit down heavily on one of the rattan chairs in reception. I miss my best friend so badly. I wish I felt as angry with her as she does with me, instead of this awful sadness.

"A swim," I say out loud. "You need a swim to sort out your head."

If nothing else, I need to NOT be in a hotel lobby talking to myself like a mad woman.

The pool is crawling with kids. Big ones, little ones, and my brothers. I move as far away from the action as I can and slide into the clear blue water.

Bliss.

My hair will go super-frizzy but I don't care. I do a couple of lengths before turning on to my back and staring up at the deep blue sky, floating like a starfish and enjoying the warmth of the sun on my face.

Peace

at

last. . .

There is an enormous splash that half-drowns me. I rise to the surface coughing and spluttering, to see a very large lady floundering beside me, gasping like an elephant seal.

"HELP!! Those two little devils pushed me in!"

Two little boys are giggling like imps on the side

of the pool, their eyes gleaming with mischief, as a lifeguard in a bright yellow shirt runs towards them with a face like thunder. Or maybe it's just a face that's trying really hard not to laugh. It's hard to tell the difference.

I'd like to make it clear that the imps are not my brothers.

Nor will they be my brothers until we are all back in Mum and Dad's suite and I can yell at them in private.

LOUDLY.

Leaving Jake and Alex to their fate, I swim over to help the spluttering lady. Half the people in the pool have had the same idea. She's pretty big and clearly doesn't do much swimming, so we need all the hands we can get.

Man. When is this holiday going to get *relaxing*?

Jake and Alex aren't exactly flavour of the month at dinner. "I've never been so embarrassed in my life!" Mum is hissing. She can be pretty scary when she's angry.

Dad is stifling a chuckle as he helps himself to a coffee top-up. "Apart from when Jake flipped that lady's skirt over her head in the supermarket last week."

"Not helpful, Bernie!"

Just then Tina makes a dramatic limping entrance. When she realizes that I'm the only one who has noticed, she goes out and comes in again, limping a little bit harder.

"What happened to you, Tina?" asks Dad.

"I got stung," Tina announces. "By the most whopping jellyfish you've ever seen. It was the size of a submarine."

"Swag," says Jake.

"Nasty," says Dad.

Tears are welling in Tina's eyes. "I'm not enjoying this holiday at all," she says, sniffing. "And I *still* can't get any reception on my phone!"

"The hotel are fixing their Wi-Fi security before a VIP guest arrives," Mum says. "It'll be back online soon."

I zone out at this point. Something very interesting has just walked into the dining room, in the shape of Jeff the Bongo Boy.

13

Monday 6 p.m. (Tuesday 4 a.m. in Glasgow)

He still has his bongos tucked under his arm. I wonder if he ever puts them down. I find myself hoping that he will start drumming right here and now. How cool would that be?

I'd get up from the table and walk over...

"Hi, Jeff," I say, all cool and collected and not talking about pee at all. "I never told you I could sing, did I?"

I start improvising a song over his beat. Jeff is totally amazed, but he keeps drumming because he knows the music mustn't stop. The rhythms grow the more I sing.

Jeff and I draw inspiration from each other like two plugs in the same electric socket.

We make everyone jump up from their tables and they start to dance like wild things. And when we bring our song to an end, the room stamps and cheers and Jeff looks into my eyes and says. . .

"You're staring at that boy like a lovelorn sheep."

And just like that . . . I'm back at the table with my family.

"I'm not," I protest, tearing my eyes reluctantly away from Jeff and making a big show of helping myself to a bread roll. "I was just . . . thinking about stuff and he happened to be in my line of vision."

"Right," says Tina, unconvinced. "Who is he? He's cute."

"Jeff." I lean my chin on my hand a little dreamily. "I talked to him in reception today. He was really cool."

"He was playing those bongos on the beach, wasn't he?" Tina says. She suddenly looks horrified. "Did he see me jumping around in the water and yelling like an idiot when the jellyfish got me? I bet he did. I bet he was laughing, the same as the beach ball boys. Did he mention me?"

Peeing. We talked about peeing. No, actually, *I* talked about peeing. (Honestly, that conversation will haunt me for YEARS.)

"I just said hi," I lie.

Tina cranes her neck, scanning the room. "I wonder what he's doing here?"

"Having a holiday?" I say.

Across the table Jake is weighing a bread roll in his hand and looking mischievously at Mum and Dad.

"Don't you dare, Jake," Mum warns.

Maybe if I'm lucky, my family will vanish. Some hope.

"But he's by himself. Who goes on holiday by themselves?"

I realize that Tina has a point. I look at Jeff again.

What *is* he doing here? If he lives on the island, why is he eating in our hotel? And if he's on holiday, where are his family, or his friends?

Jake has switched the roll to the other hand, looking way too gleeful for comfort.

Mum is already half rising from the table. "Bernie, talk to your son." Her voice sounds strained.

Dad fixes Jake with one of his pinpoint stares. "Put it down, Jake."

Ignoring the unfolding food drama, Tina nudges me. "Go and say hello," she says. "I dare you."

I freeze.

Dreaming about approaching Jeff and actually *doing* it are two completely different things. Tina grins at the look on my face.

Jake puts the roll down. Mum's shoulders relax. And then Alex reaches across, grabs the roll and lobs it at the massive fruit display on the buffet table.

Our entire table falls silent as we all watch the roll hit the big pineapple on the top perfectly. I swear, that child would clean up at a coconut shy.

We stare in horror at the cascading fruit avalanche that follows. Waiters rush from all sides to scoop up the rolling melons and strawberries and grapes.

"May I have your attention for a moment,

please?" Dad says, standing up to address the other diners, who are all watching our table with extreme disapproval. "My sons have something they would like to say to you all."

I've never seen Dad look so cross.

Tina and I both sink down in our chairs and make ourselves as small as possible.

"Sorry," Alex says in a scared voice.

"It was him," Jake adds. "Not me."

"I'm so embarrassed I can't even move," groans Tina as Mum and Dad march the boys out of the dining room. "I'm going to stay on this chair for the rest of the week."

As normal chatter finally returns to the room, Tina sits up again.

"Is Bongo Boy still here?" she asks. "Do you think he saw that?"

"*Everyone* saw that," I tell her.

Jeff has finished his meal. Tina and I watch as he scoops the bongos under one arm and heads out to the lobby.

Tina watches Jeff's retreating back. She grins

at me mischievously. "Are you thinking what I'm thinking, little sister?"

I totally know where she's going with this.

"Operation Follow That Boy?" I ask with excitement.

Tina nods. "We have to be really subtle though. Him thinking we're a couple of stalker fangirls on top of this evening's pineapple catastrophe is all we need."

Subtle is good. I don't want to throw myself at him, after all. I just want to know what he's doing here. And whether maybe he'd like to try a little jamming. With me.

But by the time we reach the lobby, Jeff has already disappeared.

Tina looks panicked. "We can't have lost him already!"

I nod at the entrance door which is sliding shut. "We haven't."

The evening is as warm as a summer's day and the air is scented with night jasmine. The moon is full and huge over our heads. Perfect conditions for a bit of boy-stalking.

"There," Tina hisses, pointing at a figure loping across the emerald-green lawn towards the road. "Go!"

We run from bush to bush, hiding and – I'll be honest – giggling quite a lot. We probably look ridiculous. But we have the scent of the hunt in our nostrils. Bongo Boy isn't getting away.

"There's nothing out here except that big maintenance shed by the car park," Tina whispers as he keeps moving towards the road. "Where's he going?"

"Maybe he's going to his car," I say.

I hope he's not. I'm all for tracking the guy, but bring a car into it and it's game over.

Tina suddenly stops dead so that I cannon into her back.

"He's going into the shed," she says in astonishment. "Do you think he's a maintenance guy?"

I can't imagine many maintenance guys get to eat their dinner in the hotel restaurants. But Jeff is definitely going into the shed, and pulling the door closed behind him.

"Maybe it's not a maintenance shed," I say, in a flash of inspiration. "There's a window there. Come on."

As we get closer, we drop to the ground and wriggle along the grass commando-style. (Way more pleasant than doing it in the school corridor!) There are voices coming from inside. It sounds like quite a party.

"Take a look," Tina hisses as we reach the little flower bed beneath the shed window.

"I'm going to," I hiss back. "Keep your hair—"

Someone inside plays a heavy chord on an electric guitar. Adrenaline courses through me as someone adds a bass and some keyboard. That distinctive Hawaiian ukulele sound next. And finally ... bongos. Wild horses wouldn't drag me away now. I pull myself up on the window sill with Tina at my feet and peep over the high-set window ledge.

"Well?" Tina says impatiently.

"Shh." My nose is pressed hard to the glass. "I'm trying to listen."

The sound is starting to build into a more

recognizable ensemble piece now: jazzy and well-paced with a strong Hawaiian vibe. I can see five people: Jeff on his bongos, a guy with long dreads on the guitar, a pink-haired girl on a little uke, a small dude in a big hat on the bass and a girl on a keyboard.

Then my heart stops. There are mics everywhere. Wires. Headphones. And at the far end of the room, a glassed-off booth with what looks like a mixing desk. I've seen this place before. In my dreams, night after night.

"It's a *recording studio*, Tina," I say in ecstasy, pressing closer to the window than ever. "Oh my gosh, I have to get a better look. Can you give me a leg-up?"

Tina links her hands so that I can step on her palms.

"Now lift me, OK?" I say, still drinking in the scene inside.

She lifts me so suddenly that I shoot into the air, bang my hands against the window, knock the whole thing open – and fall right inside with my arms waving like I'm guiding a plane on to a runway.

14

Monday 8 p.m. (Tuesday 6 a.m. in Glasgow)

I hit the floor, arms outstretched, do a perfect forward somersault and end up flat on my back, staring up at a circle of concerned faces. Oops.

What do I do now? I wasn't prepared to get *this* close to the action. Thank goodness I'm wearing shorts. A skirt would have *really* spelled a problem. (Not that this isn't a problem – it's just not a knicker-flashing problem.)

"Where did you come from?" says the pink-haired uke player.

"Are you OK?" asks the guy with dreads.

"Don't worry, I know her," says Jeff, peering down at me. "Hi, Storm. That was quite an entrance."

I decide to make the best of things.

"Hi, Jeff," I say, as brightly as I can manage. "I just thought I'd drop in, ha ha!" (It sounded better in my head.)

"But where did you come from?" repeats Pink Hair.

I clamber to my feet with as much dignity as I can manage, doing my best not to trip across any of the cables snaking over the floor.

"I, er – your window. . ." I gesture feebly at the open casement. "I'll just shut it, shall I?"

Tina isn't there. I hang over the sill and peer down into the bushes in case she's down there pretending to be a rock or something. Nada. She's left me in the lurch. This was her idea, and now she's run away and left me to my fate.

"Are you planning on diving out again?" asks Jeff at my shoulder.

I spin round, clattering the window shut behind me.

"Um, maybe?" I say, giggling out of pure nerves. "I'm really sorry about that. It wasn't exactly planned. But I heard your music and I guess I couldn't stop myself?"

Not cool, Storm! I can see Belle right now, her head in her hands as she shakes with laughter at what an idiot I am.

"You're into music?"

"Does Kanye love Kanye?" I say. "I'm totally, madly, *crazily* into music!"

"What stuff do you like?"

I can't believe Jeff is interested. I feel a bit breathless. Maybe I don't mind so much that Tina's left me here after all.

"Um, where do I start? Ivy Baxter, Ella Fitzgerald, Earth, Wind and Fire, Elton John... Anything with *heart*, you know?" I thump my chest so hard to demonstrate my passion that I make myself cough.

"You wanna hang out and listen to us for a while?" says Jeff. "I can't promise Earth, Wind and Fire, but we make a good sound."

I stare at him. "Did you just invite me to hang

out?" I ask. You know, just to be sure that I'm not dreaming.

Jeff waves at a collapsing sofa in the back corner of the room. "It's fine if you want to listen. Take a seat."

"Do we get an introduction, Jeff?" asks Dreads.

Pink Hair is Suze. Dreads is John-Henry. The big hat on bass is Ofir and the girl on keyboards is Naomi.

"Great name," says Ofir, twanging the strings on his bass and grinning at me. "Thunder Storm. Welcome to the band."

"If only!" I say, and then I laugh. I sound hysterical, I know, but I can't seem to stop. I can't believe I'm in a real recording studio with these guys – a proper band.

"Take a seat?" Jeff says again.

I scurry to the back of the room and plop myself on the sofa. I'm determined not to be a nuisance in case they tell me to leave.

"OK," says Jeff. 'Dreamin' Big', from the top."

Suze glances at the door.

"There's no point waiting for her," says Ofir, noticing Suze's glance. "She'll come when she comes."

"*If* she comes," adds John-Henry.

I wonder who they're talking about.

"Suze, take the vocal for now," says Ofir. He has a lovely voice, like thick treacle.

My whole body reacts as Jeff counts everyone in with the mellow bongo beat. Every hair on my head stands up straight. My skin feels alive. I can sense every blood cell whooshing in and out of my heart and lungs, perfectly in rhythm with the song.

"Dreamin' big," Suze starts, "dreamin' loud... You wanna go where dreams go, where dreams go, out and proud. Up to the sky, no reason why, just dreamin', dreamin' big..."

Suze keeps messing up a really easy part in the middle eight. I'm itching to jump up and sing it for her. It's not hard, it just needs ... more than she's giving it. It's not long before I realize that the missing "she" they were just talking about is probably the vocalist.

))

Wait. What? They are missing their *vocalist*?

"Nice one, Suze," says John-Henry at the end.

"Liar," says Suze, with a wry strum on the strings of her uke.

I realize that I have stood up.

"I can sing," I blurt.

I can see the band exchanging "Uh-oh, who let the wannabe in?" looks.

"Sure you can, Thunder Storm," says Ofir. "School choir, right?"

I flush. "No! Well, yes. But other stuff too. R and B stuff." I hum a part of the song Suze just did.

"We could try her," says John-Henry.

I want to kiss John-Henry and his lovely, lovely dreads.

"Are you kidding?" Suze snorts. "The chick's barely out of nappies."

The prize is so close, I can almost close my fingers on it. I can't let this moment pass.

"I can," I insist a bit more loudly. "Just let me have a go. Please?"

Jeff laughs and shrugs. "What have we got to

lose?" he says to the others. "You think you can remember the words, Storm?"

The lyrics are already engraved on my heart. I close my eyes and take a breath.

"Dreamin' big," I start, "drea-eamin' loud. . . You wanna go, oh you wanna go where drea-ea-eams go, whoa . . . out and proud. Up to the sky, no reason, no-o-o-o-o reason why-ee-why-ee-why. . ."

"Look out," says Suze. "Mariah Carey is in the building."

"Shut up, Suze," says Jeff. He's looking at me with fresh eyes. "She's good. Wanna go again, Storm? With the rest of us this time?"

My heart is going at a thousand miles an hour. This is my chance. It's me and the band and the music, in this hut, amid the scents and sounds of the Hawaiian night. I will remember this moment *for ever*. My whole body feels like it's going to explode with excitement.

"Sure," I say, as nonchalantly as I can. "Let's do it." Suddenly I feel alive. Like this was my sole purpose on earth: I was born for this. I stretch out my shoulders to calm my nerves. I close my eyes and take three deep breaths, feeling my entire being drifting slowly but surely into my ultimate comfort zone. I am ready.

15

Monday 10 p.m. (Tuesday 8 a.m. in Glasgow)

I think I may be the only person in the world who can fly. I am running back across the hotel grounds so fast that my feet are hardly touching the ground and I know that if I open my arms out I will take off and loop-the-loop through the sweetly scented night like a crazy owl. In fact, I might just try it. . .

OK, so maybe not flying exactly. But I never knew I had so much power in my legs. This whole evening has flooded my body with electricity. I am a living battery.

The moment when Suze started smiling at me was a definite high point. *"You're not bad, kid. I might even say you're good."* Ofir was adorable once he got past the school choir thing. John-Henry had the most perfect smile in the world. And Jeff. . .

"Are you free tomorrow, Storm? You wanna lay down 'Dreamin' Big' with us, see how it sounds?"

I'm going to record with a real band. They want me on vocals. *Me.*

Maybe missing the National Choir Finals isn't so bad after all.

I launch into a pirouette of excitement. Because I am travelling at speed, it goes a bit wrong and I crash sideways into an oleander bush. The scent is so gorgeous and my mood is so happy that I actually wonder if I've actually died and gone to heaven.

"What was that noise, Rico?"

I sit up, spitting out leaves at the familiar voice.

"Rico," my big sister says again. "Are there any wild animals in Hawaii?"

She sounds close. Really close. Like, on-the-other-side-of-this-bush close. And Rico? Who's Rico?

"No wild animals unless you count me," says a voice with a lovely American twang.

Tina giggles. "Tell me again what you thought when you saw me on the beach today."

"Like you were a beautiful princess in pain."

Rico must be one of the beach ball boys. How long since she left me to my fate this evening? Two hours maybe? Gotta give her credit, my sister works fast. I don't know whether this situation is annoying or funny. (I've got to admire her, actually. Restoring princess status after that episode with the jellyfish cannot be easy.)

"It was sooo painful," Tina agrees. "I really thought I was going to die."

"I'll kiss it better."

There is a gross squelching sound.

"Oh my gosh, Rico, that is my *foot*..."

Tina sounds half appalled, half thrilled. I snort with laughter, then quickly cover my mouth with my hands.

The kissing noises stop.

"There *is* someone there, Rico," Tina says, a little higher this time. "Come out, whoever you are! I don't know if you get some kind of thrill spying on people—"

I step out of the bush, brushing a few more random twigs off my legs. Tina looks horrified to see me. And I suddenly know just how to get my sister back for her little abandonment stunt tonight.

"Storm?" she gulps. "What are you doing here?"

"Hey, sis," I answer sweetly. "Mum and Dad will be very interested to hear what you've been up to tonight." I gaze down at Rico, who is still on the grass with his hand wrapped around my sister's foot. Urgh. Rather him than me. "Nice to meet you, Rico. I'm Storm. Tina's much nicer sister."

"Er, pleased to meet you, Storm," says Rico. He sounds a bit awkward. I would sound awkward too, if someone caught me smooching a person's icky toes.

"You won't tell Mum and Dad, will you?" Tina pleads.

I make a show of examining my nails.

"Seriously, Storm, they will ground me for the entire *week*. And he was only kissing my foot anyway."

"I noticed."

Tina looks even more awkward than Rico now. "And I'm sorry for leaving you the way I did tonight. I panicked."

"Hmm." I'm really enjoying myself here. "That was possibly the most embarrassing moment of my life so far, and there's plenty of competition. I'm not sure you deserve to be let off the hook so easily."

"Pleeeease, Storm." Tina tries again. "Don't tell Mum and Dad. They've got enough to worry about with Jake and Alex."

I give a big sigh. "What," I say, "is it worth?" (This should be good.)

"You can borrow any of my clothes," Tina says. "My make-up too."

"Your Pacific-blue nail varnish?"

Tina rubs her head. "You drive a hard bargain. Fine, my Pacific-blue nail varnish as well. For goodness sake, get *up*, Rico."

"You still owe me big time," I remind my sister as I drag her away from the boy and the bushes and march her towards the hotel.

"I know," Tina says. "I'll make it up to you somehow. How did you get on with the band anyway?"

I'm bursting to tell *someone* about my evening, but Tina doesn't really deserve good news right now.

"It was . . . interesting," I say. Which is, of course, true.

An entire army of hotel staff have gathered in the lobby. For a moment, I wonder if Mum and Dad have assembled a search party for me and Tina. The Hawaiian clock above the reception desk says ten o'clock. Oops.

". . . absolutely one hundred per cent," the hotel manager is saying as he marches up and down in front of the staff with his hands behind his back.

"This visit could spell disaster for the hotel unless everything runs like clockwork and the premises are spotless. Spotless, do you hear?"

Not a search party, then. Phew.

"I wonder what the manager is getting so stressed about?" Tina says as we head for the lift.

"Sounds like they're having an inspection tomorrow," I say.

Tina sighs and presses the button for our floor. "It would be way more interesting if a president or some VIP was coming to stay," she says.

Mum and Dad are both standing in the middle of our room when we open our door.

"Where have you been?" Mum demands. "I thought you'd be back an hour ago!" She fixes Tina with a fierce stare. "And did I see you outside with a boy a short while ago, Valentina?"

Tina turns green. I jump to the rescue, because that's what sisters do. (Plus, I've got to earn that nail varnish.)

"Tina was with me," I say.

"And who were *you* with?" Dad enquires.

"I was with a band." It sounds so cool and unbelievable, even as I'm saying it.

"Storm's telling the truth," Tina says, relieved that at least part of what we're telling Mum and Dad isn't a pile of porkies. "We followed this guy from the hotel and—"

I can't keep it in any more.

"—and it was *amazing*!!" I squeal. "There was this girl called Suze who wasn't keen on us dropping in at first – she has pink hair – and Ofir thought I was just a little school-choir kid and Naomi didn't say anything but John Henry and Jeff were lovely and then I discovered that their vocalist hadn't turned up and so I offered to sing with them and now we're doing a recording!"

My family and Belle are pretty much the only people I know who understand me when I ramble with excitement like this.

"You're doing a recording?" Mum repeats.

"With a band?" Dad says.

Tina looks just as stunned as my parents, only

she can't say anything because, of course, she was supposed to have been there too.

"Yes!" I squeal in bliss. "Isn't that the best thing you've ever heard?"

"What's their name?" Dad says.

"Wewehi!"

Dad looks astonished. "They're called Wee-wee?"

Tina giggles. For a big sister, she is very immature. I repeat the band's name, giving it the special Hawaiian inflection that John-Henry showed me. "Wewehi, Dad. Try and be a bit more Hawaiian, will you?"

"We saw the bongo player on the beach," Tina supplies. It's about the only fact she knows.

"They play really great music, sort of funky with a Hawaiian beat," I say. "And their lead singer didn't turn up so they invited me to sing instead."

Dad turned to Tina. "Sounds like your sister did well."

"She was great," says Tina brightly. "Seriously. The best I've ever heard her sing."

"When is this recording?"

I'm not sure I like all these questions.

"Tomorrow," I say cautiously. "Why?"

"Because I'm going to come with you."

My jaw clangs open in horror. Bringing Dad to the studio will confirm what Ofir and Suze already think: that I'm nothing but a kid. I've only just started proving that I'm way more than that. Having Dad and his eternal coffee mug chaperoning me will send me right back to square one!

"This isn't parents' evening," I manage to say. "These guys are *professionals*. Can't you see how uncool it would be if I brought you?"

"If you want to record with these people," Mum chips in, "then your dad has to go too. You're thirteen years old, Storm. We aren't leaving you unsupervized with a group of musicians we've never even met. What time do they want you?"

I wonder whether to lie. But Dad is watching me very carefully, and I know he'll spot the fib right off. If I don't tell him the truth, he'll only stalk me and then pop up at a really embarrassing moment. (Yes,

I'm struggling to think of a more embarrassing thing than actually taking him, but trust me – he would have NO trouble thinking up something worse!)

"Two o'clock tomorrow afternoon," I say reluctantly.

Dad rubs his hands. "Excellent," he says. "I can't wait."

Tuesday 11 a.m. (9 p.m. in Glasgow)

I don't peel my eyes open until eleven o'clock the following morning. For a moment I can't remember where I am as I blink at the bright sunshine pouring through the gap in my curtains. Then it all comes flooding back.

I'm doing a recording. Yay!

In Hawaii! Whoo!

Dad's coming too! Groan!

On the grand scale of things, I guess the recording thing trumps the dad thing. I'll just have to make the best of it. Maybe try and give Dad the slip at the last minute. I cunningly didn't tell him where the studio is.

I lie back on my comfy pillows and stare at sun-dappled ceiling as my brain whirs through the momentousness of the day ahead. Tina has already gone, perhaps to breakfast or perhaps to more foot-smooching with Rico. Mum, Dad and the boys will be long gone as Jake and Alex tend to wake up with the little birdies. I URGENTLY need to discuss important matters like what to wear to a recording session and *there's no one here*. What I wouldn't give right now to be able to talk to Belle! I have so much to tell her, even if she still hates me and goes "lalalala" during our whole phone call.

I suddenly sit upright. I have remembered something that Dad said yesterday. Something about a spot by the fountain in the spa where he and Mum had been able to pick up a signal.

A connection! The internet! Conversations, Twitter, Instagram!

In a flash I am up and running for the bedroom

door. Quick swerve back to my wardrobe for some clothes (kind of important), drag them on, then heading for the bedroom door again. Back-pedal to the bathroom because, yeah, teeth and face, race for the bedroom door a third time and just remember to grab my key card before slamming the bedroom door behind me. Then it's back into the room because, oops, PHONE (which has been in my bedside drawer for twenty-four hours because I have got used to living caveman-style), and out into the corridor again – SLAM – then in again for one last hair-tease and dab of make-up and out – SLAM – aaand back because I have got odd shoes on (how?) and out one more time – SLAM – and in the lift, panting slightly.

I would give a cuckoo clock a run for its money.

The spa is right at the front of the hotel, where guests can enjoy the sound of the sea as they lie there with hot stones on their backs or mud masks on their faces. Everything is super quiet here, as the bamboo-covered walls are lined with extra soundproofing to mask the hot-stone screams.

(I would scream. You would scream too, right?) Listening carefully for the sound of a fountain, I munch quietly on the warm bread roll that I snaffled as breakfast was packing up, tiptoe past treatment rooms named after Hawaiian plants – Mokihana, Lokelani, Kaunaoa – until I am on the small patio dotted with canvas recliners and big parasols. The sound of running water from the little fountain in the middle is music to my ears.

I turn on my phone and stare at it eagerly.

Nothing.

I wave it to the left, and then to the right. Zip. I stretch my arm into the air. . . One bar of reception. Yessss!!

The moment I bring the phone back down, the bar disappears.

The only thing for it is to scramble on to one of the patio tables.

BEEP, says my phone at once.

BEEP.

BEEP. Email.

BROOP-BROOP. Text.

BROOP-BROOP, BWAAA. Instagram.

BWAA, BWAA, BWAA.

DING-DONG.

DING-DONG.

DING-DONG. Twitter.

BLIING.

BLIING. Facebook.

My phone plays an entire symphony of beautiful beeps, bwaas, broops, ding-dongs and bliings and I've never heard anything so magical. At last, I am connected.

I scan my list of messages.

Nothing from Belle.

Swallowing the lump of disappointment that has risen in my throat, I force myself to concentrate on the rest. Two texts from Jade. An Instagram from Bonnie. Five calls, twelve texts, four Instagrams and nineteen tweets from . . . you guessed it.

Colin Park @iamcolinpark
@stormhall_14 The state flower of Hawaii is
called the pui aloalo

Colin Park @iamcolinpark

@stormhall_14 Hawaii was first called the Sandwich Islands after the Earl of Sandwich who invented the sandwich #sandwich

Colin Park @iamcolinpark

@stormhall_14 Hawaii's Mauna Kea volcano is taller than Mount Everest if you measure it from the seabed

Colin Park @iamcolinpark

Hey @stormhall_14 hope the leis are delicious *checks that leis are food*

Twitter is bad enough, but Instagram and Facebook have gone entirely mad since I went away. I never realized how difficult it is to keep up when your phone has been turned off for two whole days. I'm doing my best, but nothing makes sense. I'm so far out of the loop that my roller-coaster car is now parked by the toilets.

I try not to get too stalkerish over Belle's

profile, but I can't help it, scrolling madly through her pictures. I feel a wave of relief when I find one of her and me messing around in the park a few days before I left. It reminds me that we did have a friendship once, before I messed things up with my whole Little Miss Diva thing. If she really hated me, she would have deleted every single picture with her and me in, right? This is fixable. It *has* to be.

I swipe the photos along a bit further, to see what's been happening in my absence. And I see. . . I see. . .

My phone slides from my hand, bounces on the table and lands millimetres away from the fountain. I stare down at the picture on my screen as if from a great height, rather than just the smallish height of the table.

Belle has posted a picture of herself with Emily and Gwen Douglas.

"You need to leave now, Miss."

I scramble off the table, reach for my phone and gabble, "Sorry, I just need one more minute. . ." at the girl with the neat black braid and the white coat who has appeared on the patio. I've lost reception again. I try to climb back up on to the table again, but the spa girl gets in the way.

"I'm sorry, Miss, but we need to close the spa for a private booking."

My nightmare has come true. Belle and the Hockey Horrors are new BFFs.

"Um," I say, my brain working frantically for some kind of alternative explanation for the photo now burned for ever on to my brain. "Yes, but do you mind—"

"I'm really sorry," repeats the spa girl. Her voice grows steelier. "But you have to leave. Now."

I put my phone in my pocket and walk slowly back down the spa corridor. A lot more white-coated staff have appeared, herding the guests out of the spa like sheep. No one looks very happy about it. I get a flashback to the lobby last night, and the strange feeling of expectancy in the air.

"*Well*," says one of the guests as the black-haired girl shuts the door behind us. At least I think that's what she says. It's hard to understand her through the heavy mud mask she's still wearing.

"Guess what?" says Dad when I get back to the suite. "We've found a hub in the TV cabinet!"

Tina waves her phone at me from the comfort of the armchair. "Ta-da!" she says.

"Oh, and apparently someone famous has just arrived at the hotel," Dad adds, as Jake and Alex zoom from the balcony, do three circuits of the room and zoom out again shouting something about sharks.

Tina sits up. "I *knew* it wasn't just a normal staff meeting in the lobby yesterday," she says in excitement. "Who is it?"

"I heard it was a politician," says Mum.

Dad shakes his head. "*I* heard it was a film star."

I think about the weirdness in the spa. "I think they might have booked in for a hot-stone massage this afternoon," I say. "They just kicked everyone out of the spa." It makes sense. Film stars do that kind of thing all the time.

"Did you see who it was?" Tina asks eagerly.

I shake my head. My sister grunts with annoyance and returns to scrolling through her phone. As Mum and Dad round up Jake and Alex to take them to the beach, I settle down on my bed to do the same.

There's loads of chat about the National Choir Finals, and photos from Daniel McCready's fourteenth birthday party, and a lot of pictures of Glasgow in the rain. I brood over Belle's new rash of Facebook pictures, beaming at the camera and posing in clothes that she probably bought out shopping with the Hockey Horrors.

I decide to upload a few of my own to prove that I'm having a good time too, thanks very much. But of course, I haven't been taking my phone out with me so I don't have any pictures yet. I settle for a mirror shot of me pulling a face and pointing at the Wi-Fi in the TV cabinet.

Instagram, we have a *lot* to catch up on.

Paradise just got an upgrade! #Hawaii

I change into my yellow bikini and grab my bag. Then I click idly on Colin Park's Twitter account. There's a lame profile pic of him plus a background shot of some physics books on a shelf. He really knows how to make himself look cool. I wonder if he's noticed how I haven't followed him yet?

Maybe it's time that changed. He's the only one who's been trying to talk to me, after all. I click his follow button. He won't think it's weird, me following him now, right? He won't think I fancy him or anything?

I unfollow at once.

Urgh, Storm, enough. Just follow the boy already! This is the twenty-first century. I follow Alexa Chung and I don't fancy *her*.

Follow button. Facebook friend request. Click. Click. Done. I put my phone by my bed and start pulling together the rest of my things for the pool.

DING-DONG.

Colin Park @iamcolinpark

@stormhall_14 Been eaten by a shark yet?

Storm Hall @stormhall_14
@iamcolinpark Bikini'd up and heading for the
pool. What time with you?

Colin Park @iamcolinpark
@stormhall_14 Bedtime. Teddy says goodnight!

Storm Hall @stormhall_14
@iamcolinpark Back away from the soft toy, Park
#weirdoalert

Colin Park @iamcolinpark
@stormhall_14 Teddy vvv offended. Talked to
Belle yet?

I chew my lip.

Belle will be going to bed right now. She'll be
sleepy and maybe not so mad at me. I need to talk to
her so badly about the whole band thing that I think
I might spontaneously combust at any moment. I

DM her before I can think too hard about it. Then I shove my phone deep into my bag and hurry out of the room, telling myself I'll be fine if she doesn't answer. Really, I will be absolutely fine.

17

Tuesday 2 p.m. (Midnight in Glasgow)

I'm back in my room at two o'clock. One hour to put together an outfit that will rock Jeff and his band and show them some serious pop-star credentials. It shouldn't be hard, as I only have what I brought on holiday instead of half a room's worth of clothes squeezed into every drawer and cupboard I own. Oh, and Tina's stuff too, of course. I'm not about to forget our Rico deal *that* quickly.

Playsuit, co-ords, maxi skirt? Bohemian fringed midi skirt with my Topshop crop? Obviously to show off my tummy because it's already starting to go brown. Eek, weird tan line, not going THERE. Bikini – nope. Kaftan – gross. Dungarees – wait, I brought dungarees? On purpose?

The clock is ticking towards my destiny. Why is it midnight back home? Why can't Belle just wake up and message me? Do I need to apologize more loudly?

I start again. Shorts, tee, braces. We've been here before and it looks even worse than the first time. I wrench open Tina's cupboard and dive in. Flippy white dress? Too childish. Mini kilt? Jeans? Pencil skirt?

OK, cut-offs. Cut-offs are good. Layer them up with the bikini and the mesh tee and the jacket. Yes. Gladiator sandals. YES. This is finally coming together, and not a moment too soon! I fire off a snap for Instagram and tease my hair a bit more.

"Liking the look," Dad says, coming into the room. Shall we go?"

"I can do this on my own," I start, but Dad's having none of it.

"I won't get in the way, sweetheart. I promise. I just want to meet them, OK?"

"And then you'll leave?"

Dad's eyes flicker. "Maybe," he says.

Which basically means no. What am I going to do? There is no way my dad is messing this up for me.

Inspiration strikes.

"Fine," I say. "I'll meet you at the front of the hotel in five minutes. I just have to, er . . . fix my hair one more time."

Dad heads for the lift. I give myself an evil genius grin in the mirror. The recording studio is at the *back* of the hotel, heh heh!

After waiting five minutes, I ditch the jacket and the gladiators, grab my favourite sunnies (because pop stars ALWAYS wear sunnies), and take the lift that leads to the spa and the back of the hotel. There's no way Dad will catch me n—

"Hey, Storm," says Dad cheerfully as I step out of the lift. He checks his watch, almost spilling his coffee down his shirt. "Ten minutes to walk across to your recording studio. That should do it."

I boggle at him in dismay. "How did you—"

Dad interrupts my spluttering and links his arm through mine. "Let's just say, I know my daughters pretty well. Oh, and I asked in reception where the studio was."

I walk as fast as I can across the hotel lawn in the hope that Dad might twist his ankle or fall into an oleander bush and lose sight of exactly where I'm going. No such luck. He keeps stride – his legs are longer than mine – and gabs on and on in my ear.

"You never know when this tape will come in handy. You might bump into someone useful who could listen to it. They'll be a lot more impressed than if you'd recorded yourself singing in your bathroom. How many are in this band again?"

"See for yourself," I mutter as we reach the studio.

Jeff, John-Henry, Suze, Naomi and Ofir are loitering around the studio doors.

"Hey, it's the kid," says Suze, clocking me.

"Who's the old dude?"

Inspiration strikes again. It's genius. I should have thought of it *hours* ago.

"This is my agent," I say. It sounds pretty impressive. "Bernie, meet the band."

"Pleased to meet you all," Dad says, waving his coffee at them. "I'm Storm's dad."

Suze and Ofir grin knowingly at Naomi and John-Henry.

"Great that you could join us," Jeff says. "Come in."

I have turned bright red with humiliation. All Dad had to do was go along with my genius idea. Was that really too much to ask?

At least he doesn't embarrass me when we get inside the studio. He knows the names of all the equipment, and throws around phrases like "stereo microphone technique" and "acoustic absorption" that get the band nodding in agreement. I start to relax.

There's a new guy in the studio, a kid who doesn't look much older than me with a curly afro and massive headphones slung around his neck.

"This is our producer. He's Dev," says John-Henry.

"Deaf?" says Dad in surprise as Dev exchanges fist bumps with the crew and lopes off to the mixing desk behind the glass wall at the far end of the room. "That's unusual in a music producer."

O . . . K. Scrap that bit about relaxing. Fortunately the band doesn't hear what Dad said. I start breathing again as everyone settles down. In just a few minutes I'm going to be doing a recording. This is *beyond* crazy.

"Storm sang really well yesterday," Jeff tells Dad as he adjusts the height of the big chrome microphone in the middle of the room. "She has a really mature voice."

"Yes," Dad agrees. "A bit like cheese."

Ugh. Please make this stop. As if this whole chaperone thing isn't bad enough, now he's telling Dad jokes.

"I can play keyboards if you want," Dad offers.

He wanders over to Naomi's keyboards and

plays a funky little tune. It's sort of cool, but sort of not at the same time. I don't think Naomi's that impressed.

"OK, Dad," I say briskly, stepping in. "I can take it from here."

Dad looks disappointed. "I was kind of hoping to hang out for the recording. I've mixed a few tracks in my time."

Yeah. Dinosaur tracks. "Really time for you to go now, Dad," I say, pushing him firmly towards the door.

"You'll come back later, right, Bernie?" says Jeff. "Give us your opinion on the final mix?"

Dad beams like it's Christmas. "I'd love that. Be good, Storm. See you la—"

I shut the door carefully in Dad's face, then square my shoulders and turn back to the band. All I have to do now is act like I know what I'm doing. I fire off a few snaps of the band and the equipment and me, ready to upload later. These guys may be recording the music, but *I'm* recording the moment.

"OK," I say briskly as I put my phone away. "Let's

get to work. This is the mic I sing into, right?" And I tap the big chrome thing Jeff had been adjusting a few minutes earlier.

"That's the fan," says Jeff, grinning.

I rack my brains for a piece of recording equipment that might be known as a "fan".

"As in, a fan?" Suze says, catching the look of puzzlement on my face. "Spins round, keeps us cool?"

"I knew that," I say quickly. I must not blush. *I must not blush.*

John-Henry pats the stool beside him. "Come sing with me, Storm. I want a close-up of all that grit you get into your vocal."

From John-Henry's smile, I think grit's good. I wish I didn't feel so out of my depth, but at the same time I'm so thrilled that I might take off like a rocket through the recording studio roof at any moment.

It's a live recording, so we all sing and play at the same time instead of having our parts recorded separately and mixed together later. It gives the whole thing an extra edge. This feels *real*. Super scary too. But as Jeff plays the soft bongo intro to "Dreamin' Big", my nerves begin to ease.

"Dreamin' big, dreamin' loud. . ." My eyes are closing of their own accord as Naomi's keyboards breeze in. "You wanna go, oh you wanna go where drea-eams go. . ."

Suze's remark about Mariah Carey still stings.

I rein in some of my crazier improvs and concentrate on putting my soul into the words, sharpening up the tone, plenty of grit.

"Out and proud, up to the sky, no reason, no reason why. . ."

We do six takes. I hardly notice. I'm just doing what I do. I'm just singing. Because singing is my Thing. Totally and utterly my capital-letters Thing. I don't know if we've been in this place for hours, weeks or years. I don't care. I want to keep doing it for ever.

We do three songs: "Dreamin' Big", "Dark Star" and "Honolulu Blue". Jeff murmurs encouragement between each take: knock it back here, ramp it up there. It's not long before Suze is nodding too. Even Naomi says something positive towards the end. It's only "Yeah", but it feels like the Queen's Speech. And then everyone is stopping and congratulating each other and offering a packet of biscuits round the room. I feel disorientated. Is it over?

There's a knock on the door. I'm back to reality as Dad pokes first his coffee mug and then his head into the studio and grins at everyone.

"Anything for me to hear yet?" he asks.

Tuesday 6 p.m. (Wednesday 4 a.m. in Glasgow)

Dad is welcomed like some kind of long-lost hero. It takes me a while to adjust to having him back in the room, in this world which I've had to myself for the past few hours. Flopping into the squashy sofa at the back, I check my phone for the time. Six o'clock. Four a.m. back home. I've been running on adrenaline for the last four hours, and now that I've stopped, I can feel the wall rushing towards me. My eyelids are suddenly so heavy it feels like there are weights attached to each eyelash.

The sound of Jeff's bongos suddenly fills the

room. I struggle upright and rush towards the mic again, before realizing this is the playback. The sound is huge. Bigger than it sounded live.

Then a voice. My voice. It doesn't sound anything like me. It sounds too big and confident to belong to me.

"Dreamin' big, dreamin' loud. . ."

"Sugar puff," says Dad, looking at me. "That's you?"

"I guess," I say a bit sheepishly. I feel like I just met someone I recognize but don't know at all. Then I wriggle on the sofa, feeling embarrassed by the way everyone is looking at me and really wishing Dad hadn't called me Sugar Puff.

"It's a little rough, but we've got some great material to work with," says Dev, appearing from behind his glass window with his headphones slung jauntily around his neck. "We need to iron it out in a couple of places, maybe loop it a couple of times, a bit of overdubbing, that kind of thing."

"I can help with that," Dad says at once.

He and Dev go into an insanely complicated

conversation about weighting and amplitude and things that go way over my head but seem to be catching everyone else's interest.

"The tonal balance should feel sweeter if we double the harmonic. . ."

"I'm hearing distortion, maybe gate the reverb. . ."

I've only ever seen sound engineering in action at gigs, when there is a team of guys working live behind a massive mixing desk, controlling the balance of the band you're listening to. This feels different. A bit like cheating, maybe, but in a good way. Like painting from a photograph, with all the time in the world to make it as realistic and perfect as you want.

This sofa is comfortable. I blink a few times to keep my eyes open, take a few more snaps of the band and the studio, and settle back on the worn cushions. There's not a lot I can do to help right now, not knowing too much about the technical side of things. I think about the perfect cover for our debut CD instead.

I'm the main focus of the picture, looking moodily over the horizon with the rest of the band hanging out behind me. The shoot is in Hawaii, of course. There's no point flying everyone back to Glasgow – the light would be wrong for Wewehi's sunny sound. We need rich, saturated colours: a picture postcard of paradise. We stage it, tell a little story like some of the great album covers do. We've been playing beach volleyball and I'm taking a break with the salty air on my sun-kissed hair. Obviously I'm wearing the ultimate bikini covered in shiny silver studs. There's a dog in the shot, sitting mysteriously under the net. People buying the CD are like, "So what's the significance of the dog?" The dog is significant because it once lived in an Indian cave. An international dog of mystery.

Someone is pushing gently at my shoulder.

"Storm?"

I open my eyes and stare up into Dad's face as he sits himself down with a *flump* on the sofa beside me. "You were mumbling something about dogs," he says over his latest refill of coffee. "Good sleep?"

I sit up, rubbing my eyes. "I wasn't asleep," I protest. "I was thinking."

"About dogs?"

"About the album cover," I say with dignity.

"Two hours is a long time to think about an album cover, sweetheart."

Two hours? I look around the studio. Instruments, amps, mics – everything has been tidied away.

"You looked so comfortable," Dad says, "it seemed cruel to disturb you. They told me to say goodbye on their behalf."

Oh my gosh. I fell asleep during the session like . . . like some kind of *toddler*? This is BEYOND embarrassing. (Today can just totally do one. It has gone from bad to worse, humiliation-wise.)

"I *missed* it?" I say in dismay.

"Only the technical stuff," Dad reassures me. "We didn't re-record anything without you."

The truth might be painful, but I have to know. "Did I snore?"

"I prefer to think of it as rhythmic breathing," Dad says diplomatically.

Oh, that's just terrific. I breathe surreptitiously into my hands. Snoring *plus* stinky sleep breath. Maybe I'm glad I didn't wake up in time to say goodbye after all.

"But the good news is that we've mixed the tracks and burned the CD," Dad says. "Everyone loved the results. I think you will too."

He waggles a shiny silver disc at me. I stop freaking out about rumbling like an asthmatic rhino in front of Jeff and the others and I jump up, my focus suddenly as sharp as a brand-new pencil.

"Is that it?" I grab it eagerly. The disc shimmers with all the colours of the rainbow. My first CD. It's a moment to treasure. "Will you put it on?"

The first track sways in like a palm tree. "Honolulu Blue". The song was my favourite of the three we laid down.

Honolulu blue, stay true, baby, stay true. . . Honolulu, it's you, baby, it's you. Cut me to size, Siren Eyes; Honolulu blue as blue, Honolulu you as you, I'm with ya, good as new, Honolulu blue. . .

Jeff's bongos and Ofir's bass twist lazily around each other, Naomi's keyboards and Suze's uke keeping the sunny flavour and John-Henry's guitar the beachy vibe. Listening now, it's even harder to believe that it's my voice. The whole thing sounds so lush and sweet and . . . and *professional*.

Honolulu blue, baby, sweet 'n' true. . .

It's real. I have a CD. I can now officially introduce myself as Storm Hall, professional recording artist. And this is just the start.

Next stop?

WORLD DOMINATION!

19

Wednesday 12 noon (10 p.m. in Glasgow)

It looks like world domination will have to wait until I can prise my CD from Jake's grubby little fingers. (More annoying than Colin Park Super Stalker? Little brothers who take your stuff. Totes true.)

"Give it BACK!" I roar for about the fiftieth time as my brother runs giggling into the bathroom and slams the door.

"There's no way out of there unless you're planning on climbing out of the bathroom window!"

"Don't give him ideas," Mum mutters as she gathers together a bag of stuff for the beach.

I don't answer. I am shoulder-barging the bathroom door.

"I've never needed a coffee so much in my life. . ." Dad says.

Jake peeps around the bathroom door. I pounce on him at once and wrestle him to the ground. "Give . . . it . . . BACK!" I pant.

Tina bursts into the room. She's already been in the pool this morning. I think it has something to do with Rico's part-time job as a hotel lifeguard.

"I've seen the famous person," she says breathlessly.

I look up from where I'm struggling to keep Jake under control. "Who is it?"

"I don't know," Tina says.

"They can't be that famous then," says Dad.

"Oh no, I'm sure they're mega famous," Tina replies confidently.

I sit on Jake. It's more comfortable this way and gives my arms a break.

"That doesn't make sense," I tell my sister. "If they are famous, they are recognizable. That's how fame works."

"I only saw their back," she explains.

Jake wriggles.

"Not a great anecdote, is it, Tina?" I say, sitting on Jake a bit more firmly. "'I saw a mega famous person but only from behind so maybe it wasn't a mega famous person at all.'"

"They had a leather jacket on," says Tina triumphantly. "Who wears leather jackets on hot days and sunglasses on cloudy ones? Famous people, that's who. Actors and rock stars and gangsters. And I think it's a woman because she looked tiny in between her two massive bodyguards."

"Bodyguards?" says Mum.

This is starting to sound interesting. I loosen my grip on my brother for a moment. Jake takes his chance to squirm free.

"They were both about seven feet tall," Tina goes on, pleased that she has our attention at last. "The famous person looked quite fragile in between them. Storm, you'll come on a stake-out in the lobby, won't you? We have to find out who it is."

I'm not sure I want to do any more stalking with

Tina after she abandoned me last time. I shrug, noncommittally.

"For me, Storm?" pleads Tina.

It's tempting, but there's something else I have to do first.

"Give me fifteen minutes," I tell my sister. And I head for the balcony, shutting the glass doors firmly behind me.

It's been twenty-four hours since I DM'd Belle, and she still hasn't replied. I'm going to have to face the fact that she doesn't want to talk to me ever again. But I need to tell *someone* about my CD before my head flies off my neck like a cork from a bottle of champagne. ANYONE.

I DM Colin.

Colin Park @iamcolinpark
@stormhall_14 A CD? You mean a real one?

Storm Hall @stormhall_14
@iamcolinpark Uh huh!!!

Colin Park @iamcolinpark

@stormhall_14 ☺ ☺ ☺

AWESOOOOOOOMMMEE!!!! ☺ ☺ ☺

Storm Hall @stormhall_14

@iamcolinpark My brothers keep stealing it and

playing it extra loud in the hotel!!!☹

Colin Park @iamcolinpark

@stormhall_14 There's no such thing as bad

publicity!

Storm Hall @stormhall_14

@iamcolinpark U may be right!

I hesitate before sending the message,
wondering how I should sign off. A kiss
ISN'T happening. Some kind of emoji,
maybe?

A smiley is boring.
A wink is a bit try-hard.

The Spanish lady is too weird.

Maybe a smiling cat?

It's cute and does the smile thing, but it's, well, a cat and not a person and therefore NOT ME smiling at Colin Park.

I press send. Then I wish I hadn't. The smiling cat looks really strange on the end of my message. So random. What will Colin think? Will he think I think I'm a cat? Will he think I think I'm a *smiling* cat? It's not like cats even smile, for goodness' sake. They are probably the most unsmiley creatures in the universe. AND I'm allergic to them. What if Colin thinks I like cats?

I am starting to feel a bit panicky now. What if Colin gives me a kitten or something and I have to act like I love it but I just sneeze and snot goes everywhere and I have to live with a snotty nose and streaming eyes for *fifteen years* because that's how long cats live? Calm. Down. Storm.

Storm Hall @stormhall_14

@iamcolinpark How are Emily and Gwen?

Colin Park @iamcolinpark

@stormhall_14 Gwen broke her nose on a hockey ball. Hockey ball looks worse than she does. Belle misses U.

Storm Hall @stormhall_14

@iamcolinpark How do U know?

Colin Park @iamcolinpark

@stormhall_14 Because her face is covered in bandages

Not Gwen, I think. *Belle*. Tell me about Belle! Boys can be really dense sometimes. If Belle really is missing me, why is it taking her so long to reply to my apology?

I stare at Colin's messages again and feel another twinge of anxiety about the cat thing.

"You coming on this stake-out or what?" Tina asks, sliding open the balcony door.

"Would you send a smiley cat emoji to a boy you don't fancy?" I ask.

Tina looks confused. "What?"

"Would you?"

"I don't know," Tina says. "Probably not?"

"So you *would* send one to a boy you *do* fancy?" I say in dismay. I knew I shouldn't have sent it.

"I didn't say that, Storm," my sister replies with a roll of her eyes. "Are you coming or not? I'll be in the lobby. Or maybe the pool. Famous people don't wait for stake-outs, you know."

She closes the balcony door again. It's at moments like this that I really, really miss Belle. She would understand exactly how I'm feeling right now.

"YOU'RE A DARK STAR BREAKIN' THROUGH THE DAWN." My voice bawls into the stillness. Sounds like Jake and Alex have done it again.

Is murder legal in Hawaii?

20

The answer to my murder question is, sadly, no.

My brothers have really done it now. It turns out that final blast of "Dark Star" wasn't from our hotel room at all. Jake and Alex had smuggled the CD out of our room and got it on the hotel's sound system.

The guests must have jumped out of their gently tanning skins when, instead of the waves 'n' hula music that usually seeps quietly out of the tannoys in every corner of the hotel, a funky set of bongos with accompanying bass, uke, keyboards, guitar and my vocals took over.

"I don't know how Alex got it past me," Dad says. "He must have hidden the CD down his trousers."

My CD has been in Alex's pants? *Gross*.

"But how did they get it on the hotel speakers?" Tina asks in amazement.

Mum sighs. "Alex burst into tears in the lobby, saying that he'd lost us. You know how sweet he looks when he cries. The poor reception staff rushed to help him while Jake sneaked behind the unmanned desk and switched CDs."

Tina's eyes are as wide as dinner plates. "They thought of that by themselves?"

"Apparently." Dad rubs his forehead with his hand. "I took them to apologize to the hotel manager. Again. This place isn't going to forget the Hall family for a while."

We are all silent for a moment.

I have to admit, I'm impressed by my little brothers' ingenuity. They're like a very small pair of criminal masterminds. I have a sneaking suspicion that Mum, Dad and Tina are impressed too, though Mum and Dad are mainly mad. Jake and Alex are now confined to their room, where I suspect they are watching lots of telly and probably ordering unsuitable stuff from room service.

Nothing those two do will ever surprise me again.

We're outside on the big covered deck for dinner tonight. The sound of the sea is lovely and there's a tang of salt in the air. It's quiet without the boys. You don't realize how much noise they make until they aren't there. We have lobster and salad, and flaming pancakes for dessert. (That's not swearing by the way. The waiters set fire to them like you do with Christmas pudding.)

Dad holds out his hand to Mum.

"Coffee on the beach, love?" he says.

Ewwww. And awwww at the same time. But mostly ewwww.

"Honestly," says Tina as our parents leave the table hand in hand like a pair of teenagers. "You'd think they'd have grown out of the soppy stuff by now."

Mum and Dad disappear towards the shushing shoreline. I hope when I'm old I'll be walking hand in hand with someone on a beach. Colin maybe.

NO.

Did I really just think that?

What's the MATTER with me?

As I fumble to put my brain back inside my head the right way round, Tina pushes back her chair. She beams brightly at me. "Why don't we try that stake-out? The FP – that's what we'll call the famous person until we know who she is – could be anywhere. Let's start in the lobby and work— Oh, hi, Rico!"

My sister changes completely when there are boys around. It's really irritating. One minute she has a cool plan for tracking down the bodyguard-using, leather-jacketed FP, and the next she's all breathless voice and batting eyelashes.

"Hey," says Rico. I'm one hundred per cent sure that the cheesy grin he gives Tina is one that he practises in the mirror every morning. "What are you up to?"

"Nothing," says Tina.

I sigh. So much for our stake-out. Tina looks like she's already forgotten I'm there. It's clear that I'm not wanted.

I leave them on the deck. Early bed and Twitter and Instagram and hotel TV for me. I really know how to live it up when on holiday.

Carve my life into shadows, spill your blood across the water, you're a dark star breakin' through the dawn...

It *is* dawn, by the feel of it.

Early morning anyway.

I sit up blearily and rub my eyes. The music is still playing. I thought it was a dream, but no. "Dark Star" is filling the room, which means— Oh god. Not again.

My brain flicks back to the night before. I definitely hid the CD under my pillow. Jake and Alex don't have a key card to our room. Confused, I begin to disentangle from the sheets. I catch sight of myself in the mirror over the chest of drawers: my hair is sticking straight up in the air like the crest on a cockatoo and my pink teddy-bear print PJs – don't judge me – are swivelled halfway round my torso.

Great look, I tell myself.

Suddenly, a whirlwind of teeth and hair and flip-flops blasts through the door.

"STOOORRRM!" Tina screams.

I clap my hands over my ears. Tina is always pretty full-volume, but this is nearly as loud as the music.

"I've just woken up!" I protest. "My ears aren't ready for screaming just yet, Tina. And, yes, Jake and Alex are evil geniuses. I don't know how—"

"STORM!" Tina screams again. "IT'S YOUUUU!"

"I know it's me," I say. My hands are still on my ears. "It's "Dark Star". Jake and Alex nicked it again and now they're playing it. Though I would like to know how they got through a locked hotel-room door. Maybe they abseiled in at three o'clock this morning like a pair of tiny ninjas." I squint at her. "Or, more likely, you let them in this morning when I was asleep."

Tina is practically hyperventilating. Talk about a weird overreaction.

"Storm," she pants. Her voice is at a more normal pitch now, thank goodness. "It's not... Alex and Jake didn't steal the CD."

"If they didn't," I say, sliding my hand under my pillow to check for the empty space which I know will be there, "then who did?"

My fingers close around something slim, small and square. I take my CD, safe in it's plastic sleeve, out from its hiding place and stare at it in confusion. *Spill your blood across the water...* is still blasting from somewhere.

I don't understand.

"No one stole it, Storm." Tina's voice is rising again. "You're on the radio."

I think maybe there is an ejector button hidden under the mattress which shoots me out of bed like a cannonball because I am somehow upright despite having no memory of getting that way. My blood is thundering through my veins like a herd of galloping horses.

"I'm what?" I say.

"THE RADIO!" Tina is back at full pitch again. "YOU. ARE. ON. THE. RADIOOOOOO!!"

I stare at the silent CD in my hand. Then I look

across at the radio. I can see the speakers vibrating.

"I'm on the radio," I say at last.

Tina lunges, pulling me into a hug so tight I can almost hear my ribs cracking. Something volcanic erupts inside me. I'm hugging her back – despite the fact that she dumped me for cheesy Rico last night. Radio. Song. Me. The pieces start fitting together like some kind of treasure map. There was more than one CD, of course there was. The band had the others. They must have taken it to the local radio station. *I am on the radio.* And I didn't even need the National Choir Finals to do it.

My bedroom door bangs open for the second time. Mum, Dad, Alex and Jake all fall through in a heap.

"It's you, Cornflake!" Dad says through a mouthful of coffee. "We heard it in the dining room over breakfast! It's you!"

Mum hurls herself at me and Tina and hugs us both. Jake and Alex somehow get into the tangle as well. I can feel their little arms grasping me somewhere around the knees.

"My daughter!" Dad shouts out into the corridor. "You're all listening to my daughter! How about that?"

"Dark Star," I sing above the clamour. "Taking fli-i-ght, breaking out into the night, burning me, touching you, fa-a-st and loose is what you do, dark star, da-a-ark star, whoa—"

"Shh," says Mum suddenly. "They'll say your name in a minute, Storm."

The host's creamy American voice comes in on cue. I stare eagerly at the speakers. The moment is going to be exquisite and perfect, and I want to remember it for ever.

"And that's "Dark Star", the new song from local band Wewehi with Lily Kealoha on vocals. I think we can all agree that these guys are ones to watch."

21

Lily who?

At first I think I've heard wrong. I'm listening so hard for my name that I've somehow laid a different name on the top of my own. I feel a flicker of doubt, then annoyance that I wasn't concentrating properly for my first ever radio name-check.

"Did he just say 'Lily'?" Mum asks.

I'm not the only one who heard a different name! I feel a cold stone of unease in my belly.

Tina confirms it. "He definitely said 'Lily'."

"Who is Lily?" asks Dad in confusion.

I feel like I've been hit by a truck. This Lily

person just got name-checked on MY track on MY big radio moment.

How is this possible?

"It's a mistake," I say. It has to be. That was my voice. I have a CD to prove it. It's still in my hand, from when Tina came in two minutes ago.

"Stations make mistakes like that all the time," Mum says. "They'll probably put out an announcement in a minute."

The presenter is saying something else. I shush my giggling brothers fiercely and fall beside the radio with my ear pressed to the speakers. I'm not missing another word.

"And I'm delighted to welcome into the studio Wewehi's lead singer, Lily Kealoha herself. Welcome to the show, Lily. How does it feel to hear your first track on the radio?"

I wonder if I've slid sideways into some new dimension as a stranger's voice answers the presenter's question. The voice is sweet and bacon-smoky with that slow Hawaiian thing going on behind it. Gorgeous? Yes. Mine? No.

"It's great to be here. I'm so excited to be a part of it."

"How long has the band been together, Lily?"

"We formed around nine months ago. We perform all over Hawaii and we have plans for a tour to the mainland in the summer."

"That's terrific. You have a great sound. Really unique. Do you have an album in the pipeline?"

"We'll be laying down a few more tracks over the next couple of months, getting the album together. We're hoping to release it towards the end of the year."

"And I'll be the first to hear about it, right?" The presenter laughs. "I want to be known as the guy who gave Wewehi its first airtime."

Lily Kealoha laughs back. "We'll be sure to let you know!"

I slump away from the radio and curl up in a tight ball on the rug. I didn't think it was possible to feel worse than I felt when I lost my National Choir Finals solo. But that was nothing compared to this. I feel as if I have been stabbed in the guts and the knife has been twisted round twenty times. Oh, and dipped in some kind of burning acid.

"I still don't understand," Dad says.

Tina's hands are on her hips, which is a sure sign that she's angry. This sort of cheers me up a bit. "Isn't it obvious?" she spits.

"Uh," says Dad uncertainly. "No?"

"This *Lily* is the usual singer for the band. The singer who didn't show up for rehearsal the day Storm fell through the recording studio wind— I mean, the day Storm and I followed the band and Storm sang for them for the first time."

Everyone digests this information.

"*Well*," says Mum at last. Her voice is vibrating with disapproval. "She has a cheek, claiming Storm's song like that! It's theft, plain and simple."

I get slowly to my feet. I need to talk to Belle. It's about seven o'clock in the evening back at home. Belle will know what to do. Belle will make me feel better. Belle always does.

"Storm," Mum says, reaching out her hands towards me.

"I'm OK, Mum," I say, though I'm not. "I just need a minute."

I back out of the double doors and on to the balcony, where I take five deep breaths in a row.

I text Belle.

I miss you. I'm sorry I was so horrible to you. I have to tell you the worst thing that's ever happened to me. You're the only one who can help me. IDA xxxx

Belle and I only ever use IDA in total dire emergencies. IDA isn't thrown around lightly. *I'll do anything.* She can't ignore it. She won't ignore it.

The phone screen stays blank.

She's going to ignore it.

I bite the edge of my thumbnail, staring at my screen. *Please, please, please—*

You are still an idiot but you're my idiot. What's up?

OMG I love you!!!!

I'll never fight with you

ever ever EVER AGAIN!!!!!

Get on with it. What's the IDA?

I text Belle the whole tragic tale. The stalking, the window, the trial song, the demo. The theft of my song. Everything. Her outraged reply is like ice on a burn.

BANG OUT OF ORDER!!!! Can't believe it.
Tweeting the radio station now. Track down
Bongo Brains and make him sort it out. I got your
back. xxBxx

I knew my BFF wouldn't let me down in my hour of greatest need. I feel calm again for the first time in days. Now I know what to do, the burning knife thing is starting to fade and something else is taking its place. I think it's rage.

Yup. It's rage. My whole body is shaking with it.

I feel as if the top of my head might flip open at any moment in a fountain of boiling lava, like Hawaii's Mauna Kea volcano on a bad day.

I crash back through the balcony doors. My whole family flinches at the look on my face.

"Don't do anything silly," Mum begins, but I raise my hand wordlessly and run on past her and Dad and Tina and the boys, heading for the door and the corridor and the lift. Jeff won't even have bongos for brains by the time I've finished with him.

"Storm, you can't go out like that, you're still wearing—"

Tina's voice cuts out abruptly as the hotel-room door slams behind me. I'm running down the carpeted corridor now, my fingers cutting into the CD which is still in my hand and my bare feet squishing into the carpet. The lift opens immediately, as if it understands the urgency of my mission, and I barge right inside. There's a cleaning lady in there who scuttles out in terror as I bang the lift button and fold my arms, practising my bone-melting glare in the lift mirror. The teddy bears dotted all over my pink PJs grin back at me. I dimly realize that I'm still wearing the uncoolest pyjamas in the world.

It's a measure of how furious I am that I find I don't care. (Well, maybe a bit, but not enough to go back up and change. I'm not out to impress them this time – I want justice!)

Lobby. Reception desk. My feet feel like they have wings. I pump my hands by my sides like the cop in *Terminator 2*. Past the startled doorman. Past a massive swarm of photographers who level their cameras at me in excitement and then put them down again. I'm just an enraged kid in cute sleepwear and they're obviously here for the FP. I wonder briefly whether to ask who they're waiting for and report back to Tina, but I'm too angry.

I could have been an FP if Lily Kealoha hadn't stolen my moment.

Jeff is going to wish he'd never been born.

22

Thursday 10 a.m. (8 p.m. in Glasgow)

I rocket towards the beach. The sand is hot under my feet. Thanks to a certain lack of underwear, things are – *bouncing*, if you get my drift. I fold my arms across my chest and keep running to the place where I first saw Jeff and his bongos.

I'm a vampire following the scent of human blood.

I'm snarling.

I'm snapping.

Believe me, I wouldn't want to meet me in a dark alley right now, pink teddies or not.

"Hey!" shouts someone, swinging round as I charge past. "Did your bed catch fire?"

There are people everywhere, sitting up on their loungers and gawping at me. One or two kids point and laugh. I send them a look of purest rage and run on towards the palm trees where I first laid eyes on Jeff. He isn't there. I squeal to a halt, digging my heels into the sand, sending a spray of silvery grit into the air.

Now I'm running back the way I came. Back past the laughing kids, and the gaggle of photographers. By the time I hit the lawn, my lungs are burning almost as fiercely as my anger, but I'm still not done. The recording studio is the next place to look.

Nothing. Empty and dark and silent. I press my hands to the window and gaze inside, biting hard on my lip as I remember the magic of yesterday. It can't be gone. It just *can't*.

Something bright catches my eye as I turn away from the recording studio window. Long pink hair, blowing in the breeze. The band is gathered around a black van in the car park, loading instruments through the double doors at the back.

I start running again. "Hey!" I yell. "Hey, Jeff!"

Jeff turns round to face me, bongos under one arm. I can't see Ofir because he's deep inside the van stowing amps and mics in boxes. Suze and John-Henry are already sitting in the van, John-Henry's arm hanging out of the driver's window.

"Hey," says Jeff. He looks pleased to see me. I plan to change that.

"What are you doing?" I say.

He blinks. "Packing the van. You?"

I jump into battle, feet first.

"Why didn't I get a mention on the radio this morning?" I demand, jabbing Jeff in the chest with one fierce finger. "That was MY song. Not Lily's!"

Jeff pushes my finger away. "Sorry, but it's the band's song. Not yours. Ours. We can credit who we like. Lily is our lead singer. Lily gets the credit."

And then he grins at me. Of all the reactions guaranteed to make me even madder, a grin is top of the list. I mean, seriously? (Thinking about it, it could be these flipping ridiculous pyjamas he's finding so amusing. Still. Not helping.)

"You're *grinning* at me?" I am breathless with fury. "Don't you. . . I ought to. . . That's. . ." I'm so mad I can't even speak in sentences, just the occasional blurty word.

"Don't get me wrong," Jeff adds, slinging his bongos at Ofir, who stows them neatly beside a huge amp. "We're really grateful that you stepped in to record with us. It was our last chance to lay down the track before our slot on the radio show. It was touch and go whether we'd get the song to the station in time."

"Thanks to ME," I shout. "It should have been my name on that track, Jeff. It's not FAIR."

I sound like a whiny toddler, I know I do. But I can't help it. I hear Suze laugh from the passenger seat.

"The kid's upset, Jeff," Ofir says, jumping down from the back of the van. "Maybe we should buy her an ice cream."

John-Henry throws me a sympathetic look but doesn't say anything. I am determined not to cry, even though I feel like wailing with all my lungs.

"You should have given me the credit. It's your song, but that's MY vocal, not Lily's," I spit.

I think Jeff's figured out how mad I am now. He's not grinning so widely anyway. "I'm sorry, Storm," he says. "You were great, but we have to promote the band now. Lily is our singer, so she gets the name-check. We can't confuse the fans. Finally, we have a real chance to make it. "Dark Star" is going to be huge thanks to Larry Lamorna's radio show. Do you know how few bands get that kind of coverage? Now I'm sorry but we've got to go. We have a gig on one of the other islands tonight, and we have to fetch Lily from the station and catch our flight."

Jeff jumps into the back of the van with Naomi and Ofir.

"You should be using ME at your gig!" I yell. To make my point, I brandish my CD at them as John-Henry starts up the engine with a rumble.

"You can keep the CD," Jeff says, starting to slide the van door shut. "Nice PJs by the way. See you around, Storm."

"No. . ." I start running after the van. "You can't just drive away. . . Come BACK!"

But John-Henry accelerates and I have to stop running. The last I see of Wewehi is the back of their black van sending up clouds of dust as it swerves from the car park and out of sight.

I slump down on the hot tarmac. No gig. No name on the radio. My life is officially over.

I stay like that for a few seconds. Between you and me, it's pretty uncomfortable. There are a few other people in the car park now who are looking curiously at me. Or maybe at my pyjamas. Either way, I know I can't stay like this. I can either throw myself down full-length and hammer the ground with my fists, or I can rise above the injustice of this moment, learn from it and come back better and stronger.

I am a phoenix, I think, fighting to stop my chin from trembling. *Rising from the fire. I was ashes and now I'm not.* (Although that stiff-bodied tantrum is mighty tempting right now.)

I get slowly to my feet and walk back across the

hotel lawn towards the lobby. The paps are still there. One or two of them fire their cameras at me this time. Proof of how bored they must be. I hope *those* never surface once I'm rich and famous. (Hahaha. Yeah, right. That will be the day.)

Inside the lobby, I swerve into the cool marble bathroom and rest my head against the mirror for a few moments. Then I take a step back and assess myself. Crazy hair: crazier. PJs: dusty. I turn to see what the back view is like. Not much better. All I can do is get some water into my hands, rub my face with it and push the rest through my hair in a bid to flatten it to my scalp a little. Can I improve the look? I roll up my PJ top a couple of inches to show off my brownish tummy, then tie a knot. I assess the difference. Zero.

Just the walk of shame to the lift remains. I hold my head as high as I can – it helps keep the tears away – press the button and step inside. I realize my feet are hurting.

I wonder if I can get rid of all this tension and misery and anger in one good scream. I take a breath as the doors begin to slide shut, preparing to bawl my lungs out.

A hand slides between the metal doors at the very last second.

"Room for one more?" says a voice.

23

Thursday 11 a.m. (9 p.m. in Glasgow)

As the man steps into the lift beside me – he's well dressed, I notice, in a sharp suit with a nice crisp white shirt and the gleam of gold cufflinks at his wrists – I realize something extremely important. My mouth is open and my scream is already on its way. There's nothing I can do other than try and slow it down. It's like riding your bike at full speed down a steep hill and only slamming the brakes on at the very last minute. There's the smell of burning rubber as your wheels lock and you swerve and slide all over the place before coming to a panting, adrenaline-fuelled stop right at the bottom.

"*AAA*-AAA-aaaa-um," I screech/croak/whisper. It's a truly stupid noise.

"Bless you," says the man.

He looks sideways at me with twinkling chocolate-brown eyes. I have a feeling he knows that my strangled bike-brakes explosion wasn't a sneeze.

I clear my throat. It feels raw. "What floor do you want?" I ask dully.

"Nine," he says.

That's the penthouse floor. I should have guessed he'd be a penthouse guy with his suit and gold cufflinks.

"Going up," I say.

But because I'm still trembly from the horrible scene with Jeff and my unscreamed scream, my finger hits the basement button instead.

"Funny kind of up," says the Suit in amusement as the lift goes down.

"Sorry," I mutter, flushing bright red. Who knew my day could get worse?

I press our floor, then his floor. We wait as the

lift hangs around for ever down in the gloom of the basement before realizing that we want it to go up again. Clunk. Whirr. I swear can feel its resentment.

"You were about to scream," says the Suit conversationally. "Weren't you?"

Hi. I'm Storm Hall. Not only am I a weirdo in PJs, I also scream in lifts.

"Um," I mumble aloud. "Maybe?"

"Want to give it another go?"

It's a kind offer. But there's no way I'm screaming in front of this well-dressed stranger so I shake my head. "It's gone away now," I say, even though it hasn't and probably never will.

"What was the problem?"

Everything bursts out of me like soda from a briskly shaken can. I have no idea what he makes of my mad rambling rant about radios and song thieves and mad dashes through hotel grounds in pink-teddy pyjamas, but it's such a RELIEF to be talking about this that I don't care. I have no idea how much he's taking in as the lift cranks upwards.

"... and I'm SO MAD about it that I can hardly

breathe and that's why I half-screamed just now and thanks—" I finish in one breath as the lift clunks to a stop at my floor. "For listening, I mean. If you did. Don't worry if you didn't. I just needed to say it all. You know?"

I step out of the lift and aim my CD at the bin positioned by the lift doors. But then the Suit puts his hand out, stopping the doors from closing, and says something surprising.

"Give it to me? I'd love to hear it."

"You're welcome to it," I say, thrusting it into his hands. "I hope I never hear it again."

"You're back!" Mum rushes up to me with relief written all over her face as I march inside our room and slam the door behind me. I shrug with one shoulder, which isn't easy in Mum's anaconda-like embrace.

"Did you find the band?" Dad asks as Mum finally lets go.

"Did you tell them they were scumbags?" Tina adds.

I don't want to go through it all again. I just shrug with my other shoulder, flop down on my bed and put my head in my hands. "I want to be by myself for a bit," I say through my fingers. "If you don't mind."

"We're going down for some coffee," says Dad. "I mean, lunch. Meet you by the pool later if you like?"

"I'm just going to stay here," I say.

Then I turn round and open the balcony doors, sliding them shut behind me. Flopping down on to a lounger, I close my eyes and seethe like a witch's cauldron. I stay like this for about half an hour before realizing how ravenously hungry I am. (Turns out rage gives me an appetite – who knew?) Raiding the minibar, I set out my wares on the balcony and make my way through every single item of food or drink that's available. Macadamia nuts. Sparkling water. A banana. Chocolate-covered pretzels, more water, an entire bag of salted almonds, a packet of gummy Bears, an apple, a bottle of orange juice, some large and very sticky cookies. When I pop the mini-pack of Pringles, I pretend I am sticking my finger through Jeff's bongos. POP.

In between snacks, I check my phone for updates. Before I know it, I'm googling Wewehi and Lily Kealoha.

Wewehi was formed in Oahu when singer-songwriter Jeff Johnson and his partner Suze Slimani pulled together the band's distinctive sound together with bassist Ofir Mbele, John-Henry Baptiste and Naomi Lim. Lily Kealoha joined the band three months later following contractual disagreements with the group that launched her, the Skirtz. Early Wewehi gigs were a hit on the live circuit, and the band has toured most of Hawaii. They recently recorded a number of tracks and an album is scheduled for release later this year.

"Contractual disagreements" basically means that everyone fell out. And what kind of name is the Skirtz? I pore obsessively over Wewehi's list of upcoming gigs. Pearl City, Waipahu, Kaneohe. Each name feels like a little knife in my side. All those gigs. All those opportunities. Gone for ever. (Yes. I know I am only here a week and I can hardly do a tour while I'm still at school, but . . . stop being reasonable! I'm cross!)

I eat the rest of the salted almonds in a fresh surge of fury.

The fury abates as I scroll through a list of recent tweets to Larry Lamorna's radio show. True to her word, Belle has been busy. And she's not the only one.

Belle Pace @bellemon
@lazlamorna @radiooahuwahoo Lily Kealoha is a liar liar pants on fire. @stormhall_14 is Wewehi!

Colin Park @iamcolinpark
@radiooahuwahoo @lazlamorna @hawaiiherald Wewehi are nothing w/out @stormhall_14

Jade Miller @jademilz00

@radiooahuwahoo DON'T NO TALENT WHEN U
C TALENT!!!! @stormhall_14 4EVAAAAAA!!!!

There are lots of other names contacting the radio
show to complain too; people I've never heard of that
Belle has obviously been rounding up on my behalf.
I feel a lump of gratitude in my throat. Technology
and friendship are amazing, reaching halfway around
the world to kick off at a Hawaiian radio station.

It's unbelievable and wonderful.

We all chat online for a while and I'm smiling
again. With friends like this, Wewehi and Lila
Kealoha can both take a running jump.

I'm logging off as Tina barges into the apartment.
All these dramatic entrances are starting to get
annoying.

"Ivy," my sister gasps, skidding on to the balcony.

"Have a what?" I slip my phone into my pocket.
"Forget the minibar, I've eaten everything."

"IVY," Tina says again. Her voice is squeaky like
a mouse. "VIP. Ivy."

"Try talking in sentences, Tina," I suggest. "Sentences are the foundation of civilized conversation." (After my inability to string three words together when confronting Jeff, this strikes me as particularly funny.)

Tina grabs me by the shoulders and looks deep into my eyes. "The VIP," she says, a teensy bit more slowly. "I know who it is, Storm. I just found out. It's Ivy."

Fireworks start exploding in my head. Did Tina... Did my sister just...

"Ivy?" I repeat stupidly. "As in ... Ivy *Baxter*?"

"No," Tina says, rolling her eyes. "The other mega-famous and utterly legendary Ivy. Of COURSE Ivy Baxter!"

My sister is still holding me by the shoulders. Which is just as well, because I've lost all the feeling from the waist down. If she lets go, I will crumple to the floor like a dying opera singer. The last time I saw Ivy, Belle and I were having the night of our lives at her Glasgow gig.

And now Ivy's here. In Hawaii. *At our hotel.*

"IVY!" I scream.

Tina is already pulling up her Twitter feed to show me. I pull out my phone as well.

Ivy is trending.

So is Hawaii.

Twitter is going nuts.

This is real.

News 4 Youz @news4youz

Fans going ballistic at rumours that IB will

appear in surprise Honolulu gig Sat night #Ivy

Celebrity News @celebnewsstories

Ivy Baxter rumours confirmed, more when we

have it #Ivy #hawaii

Ivy Ivy Ivy @topIvyfangirl

Follow me pls @therealIvyB U will make my life

Celebrity News @celebnewsstories

IB trademark surprise show in Honolulu Sat

night, tix selling fast #Ivy

Ivy Baxter @therealIvyB

Laterz Hawaiiii! ♥☺

↻ 6823 ★ 9450

"This is real, right?" I say, still scrolling through pages and pages of feed. It's *Ivy*, *Hawaii*, *Honolulu*, *Ivy*, *Hawaii*, *Honolulu* over and over again.

"If Twitter says it's real, it's real," Tina says. "We have to find her before she leaves the hotel for the show."

Wewehi and the humiliations of this morning are all forgotten. Ivy is the only thing that matters right now.

"What are we waiting for?" I say eagerly, my hand already on the door handle.

Tina eyes my PJs. "Er ... a change of outfit, perhaps?"

24

I'm glad someone round here is thinking straight. It was bad enough having normal people staring at my pyjamas, let alone ultimate style idol Ivy Baxter.

I change as quickly as I can. Which isn't very quickly. If we're going to meet my all-time musical heroine – SQUEEE! – then the outfit has to be *perfect*.

"Come ON," Tina groans as I throw my clothes around our room in a desperate bid for the perfect Ivy-hunting outfit. "If you don't put something on in the next five minutes I'm leaving without you."

"Give me a break, you know how important this

is," I say, diving into my wardrobe like a seagull after a fish. "Faux fur or not?"

"Anything," Tina begs. "Just put it ON."

Shorts, tee, gladiators. Faux fur on top. (I *knew* I was right to bring it.) Tease the hair, dab of make-up, squirt of perfume, GO!

There is a teensy problem, of course. Ivy is notorious about her privacy. She never does interviews. She takes paparazzi to court. No one ever knows who she's dating. She does surprise gigs in secret spots around the world at a moment's notice. She's hardly going to advertise which room she's in. I hope Tina has a plan.

"The plan is to cover every inch of this hotel like forensic scientists," my sister informs me. "Every corner, every cupboard, every bin."

"Ew," I say. I'm not sure how digging around in bins is going to help.

"OK, forget the bins. We'll start with the spa."

The spa feels totally Ivy-free and normal. There are no prowling beauticians in white coats telling everyone to leave. There's only one brief moment of excitement when Tina grabs me and points at a lady in a mud mask through a half-open treatment-room door.

"Do you think that's her?" she gasps.

"Hard to tell," I say honestly.

We're starting to attract suspicious looks, so we leave the spa and return to the lobby. Pulling up two seats, we decide to blend into the furniture for a while and just watch the comings and goings.

"The paps are getting really bored," says Tina after forty minutes of sitting very still and staring through the big glass doors at the front, where the crowd of photographers are hanging around listlessly with their huge cameras dangling around their sweaty necks.

"So am I," I say with a sigh. "My leg has gone to sleep from sitting in this chair for so long. This isn't working, Tina. We need to *talk* to people."

The reception staff seem like a good place to start. We make a quick plan, then march over like we know exactly what we're doing.

"Hi," Tina begins as I smile winningly at her

elbow. (Not literally at her elbow because that would be strange. I am *beside* my sister's elbow. Just so we're clear.) "Ivy sent us to check for any messages?"

The lady on reception has a flower behind her ear and eyes like steel traps. "Ivy who?" she says.

I glance over my shoulder, then lean across the desk. "Ivy doesn't like to cause a fuss, so if you could just give us any messages we can pass them on," I say in a low voice.

"I need a surname," the receptionist says. (Yeah, right! Like she doesn't know who we mean.)

"Baxter," I say, playing along.

She blinks ever so slightly. "There is no one at the hotel of that name."

"We all know that's not true," says Tina.

There is a brief stare-off. No one wins.

"Is there a problem?" asks the manager, popping up like a genie from a bottle.

"We work for Miss Baxter," says Tina boldly. I have to admire her nerve. "We've come to pick up any messages and deliver them to her room."

"I'm sure I don't know who you mean," he says with the sort of finality in his voice which says THIS CONVERSATION IS NOW OVER.

He pops off again. The receptionist pops off after him. Tina and I are left by ourselves.

"Plan B?" I say after a while.

Plan B involves an aimless wander around the beach, the grounds and the pool. The faux fur isn't so great out of range of the hotel air conditioning.

"I can't believe we're in the same hotel as Ivy and we can't find her," I groan as we walk back into the lobby in defeat an hour later. "We are going to be chips that pass in the night."

"Ships," says Tina.

This is hardly the moment to be correcting my figures of speech. "Whatever," I say. "This is *serious*. The paps are getting thicker by the minute. She must be here *somewhere*!"

But, of course, this is Ivy Baxter we're talking about. International Superstar of Mystery. She doesn't have to be anywhere if she doesn't want to be. We're no closer to figuring out where she is than we were two hours ago.

Tina and I return gloomily to our apartment. I need a brainwave. I have a feeling I'll think more clearly without the distraction of glorious Hawaiin sunshine, so I wriggle under my bed and try to pretend that I'm at home. It a tight squeeze and it smells different and there are a LOT of dust fairies, but it'll do.

If I were Ivy Baxter, where would I be right now?

It's obvious if I think about it. I'd be in my huge, private penthouse suite where I would have everything I needed. I'd have a deep, scented bath, and a hairstylist would come to my suite and do my hair. I'd have a manicurist too, and a stylist picking my outfit and pressing it so that it looked superstar perfect. I'd eat a light meal beside the rooftop pool and I'd laugh at all the paps, autograph-hunters and hopeful teenage fans milling around down in the heat and dust below.

"Tina," I say, with my nose pressed to the underside of my bed. "We need to go up to the penthouse floor."

Someone is knocking at the apartment door. I hear the clink of the lock as Tina opens up.

"Hi, is this your CD?" says a voice. "I totally adore it!"

I try to sit up, bang my nose on the bed, and fall back down again with a groan. The voice is familiar, somehow. Tina isn't saying anything at all, which is weird. Is this person talking about my CD? The one I threw in the bin? Wait, I didn't throw it in the bin, did I? I gave to the Suit in the lift. That voice doesn't belong to the Suit. I feel unaccountably nervous.

"Please tell me we have the right room. We've tried about five so far."

My sister speaks at last. It's hard to make out the words because she's doing her squashed-mouse impression again, only there aren't any jellyfish in our apartment.

I am getting the impression that the whole next-door room is full of people now. I am completely unable to move. I've worked out why I know this voice. I hear it almost every day, pouring through my headphones, singing fierce and wonderful songs.

Ivy Baxter is in my apartment.

"Did I say how great this CD is yet? My boyfriend gave it to me a couple of hours ago and we've been listening to it ever since. We can't get over the quality of the vocal. We've been trying to work out which room you were in for the past half an hour. What's this, the fifth room on this floor that we've tried?"

"Sixth," says the Suit. I know it's him. I recognize his voice from the lift. "Do you have a sister who wears teddy-bear pyjamas, by any chance?"

Pennies are dropping like one of those funfair coin-pusher games. *Plink, plink, plink.* The Suit is Ivy Baxter's boyfriend. WHAT? The Suit gave Ivy Baxter my CD. WHY? (It can't be that my silenced scream gave a good impression of my voice!) Ivy Baxter likes my CD. HOW? Ivy Baxter and the Suit, and who knows how many other people have apparently come into my family's hotel apartment for a chat about it. WHOA.

"I . . . yes," Tina manages to say.

There's a ripple of applause. There must be at least five people out there.

"Where is she?" asks Ivy.

I stay lying perfectly still as the bedroom door opens and shuts quietly behind my sister. Tina gets down on all fours and peers at me. Despite her berry-brown Hawaiian tan, her face somehow looks as white as chalk.

"Storm," she says. "Ivy Baxter wants to talk to you."

25

I continue staring rigidly at the bed slats. I can feel myself going a bit cross-eyed.

"Did you hear me, Storm?" says Tina after a minute. "I said—"

"I heard you."

My voice sounds thin and very far away. This is beyond embarrassing. Ivy Baxter is in my apartment, wanting to talk to me about my CD, and I am lying under the bed like an old pair of slippers.

"Seriously, Storm. Come out," Tina screams.

"I can't move," I tell my sister.

"Of course you can. You just slide out, same way you slid in. And hurry up *because there's a flipping megastar waiting in the living room.*"

"Seriously, I can't move." My nose is starting to hurt, wedged up against the bed slats. "I'm stuck, Tina."

"Oh, for the love of—"

The door opens again.

"Hey. How's it going down there?"

My heart jumps into my throat like a startled salmon at a waterfall. By turning my head ever so slightly, trying not to scrape too much skin off my nose as I go, I spot the ultimate pair of fierce boots standing in my bedroom doorway.

"Fine, thanks," I say weakly. I am talking to Ivy Baxter's boots while stuck under a bed. (Surreal, huh?)

Ivy sounds amused. "I think your sister needs a hand. I'd do it, only these pants aren't really designed for kneeling down."

Tina's clammy fingers grasp me by the wrist and pull until I pop out from under the bed like a sweaty-faced cork. I know my nose is bright red, maybe even dented with slat marks. I should have taken off the faux fur before I got under there. I feel like Oscar the Grouch.

It's only when I've stood up and brushed a bit of the dust off that I can bring myself to follow the fierce boots up the leather leggings, past the brown belly studded with rings, past the bustier and the jacket and the massive silver necklace, all the way up to Ivy Baxter's face with her slanted green cat's eyes and her tousled jet-black hair. She looks exactly like she looks in all her publicity pictures. My legs go a bit wobbly. I can't shift the feeling that I'm staring at a poster.

"You're Ivy Baxter," I say. (Well, duh! It's not my finest hour, telling a megastar her own name while covered in fluff.)

"Last time I looked," Ivy agrees. "What's your name, sweetheart?"

I literally have no idea what my name is right now.

"Storm Hall," Tina supplies. "And I'm Valentina Hall," she adds, keen not to be left out of things. "We're from Glasgow. We're here with our mum and dad and brothers on holiday. We're massive fans of your music. I'm talking too much, aren't I?"

Over Ivy's shoulder I see the Suit raising his arm and waving in my direction. Three or four other people are standing around him, looking at me too. I wonder exactly how much dust I have in my hair.

"How old are you, Storm Hall?" says Ivy. She's holding my CD, her long shiny black fingernails clutching the plastic case.

"Thirteen," I croak.

"Your voice sounds older. Is it really you on this CD?"

I raise my arms weakly in a shrug. A shower of dust sprinkles to the floor. "Um," I say carefully, "yes?"

Ivy studies me. "You have an incredible voice for someone so young."

If I had a tail, I would be wagging it super hard right now. Ivy Baxter thinks I can sing. Ivy Baxter thinks I'm incredible.

I clear my throat so I don't sound quite so much like a frog. "Um, thanks."

I'm talking to Ivy Baxter.

And Ivy Baxter is talking to me.

The megastar currently standing in my hotel bedroom doesn't seem to have noticed that my hair is on end and I'm wearing an entire coat of carpet fluff. I start to relax. I can do this. She's just a person, right? An incredibly talented and famous and gifted person but a person just the same.

"Alec tells me you've been dumped by your band?" she says.

Alec must be the Suit. He grins at me again from the living room. How much did I tell him exactly? That whole lift episode is a blank. (What can I say? Red rage: improved appetite, really rubbish short-term memory.)

"Kind of," I tell her, doing my best to unglue my tongue from the roof of my mouth. "Although they weren't really my band, to be honest. Well, they were my band for about two hours, and then for three minutes on the radio, or at least I thought they were, but then they weren't."

I'm not explaining this very well. But you should try having a serious conversation with a superstar when your entire brain is screaming with shock. It's not easy.

Ivy waggles the CD again. "Why they would dump you when you can sing like this," she says, "I have no idea."

"They dumped her because they're idiots with surfboards for brains," Tina chips in.

Ivy laughs. It's a beautiful gravelly sound. Tina turns pink with delight. If I know my sister – and I do – she's already rehearsing the anecdote in her head. *And then Ivy laughed at this joke I made...*

"The music business is tough," Ivy says. Her eyes are studying me carefully from head to toe. I find myself wondering if I should turn slowly like a chicken on a spit so she can see the whole package – but I don't. There's a major dust thing going on down my back. The only good news here is that I changed out of the PJs.

"They already had a singer," I say, trying to stay focused on the making-chitchat-with-famous-people thing. The fact of Lily Kealoha still stings like Tina's jellyfish. "I stood in for the recording because she didn't show up. She took the credit."

"Is she as good as you?" Ivy inquires. "Actually, don't answer that. I'm not interested in her."

The posse hanging out around Alec the Suit must be the bodyguards Tina saw in the hotel corridor earlier. They are just as massive as she said they were. Black T-shirts, black sunglasses, expensive watches. I wonder if I have slipped sideways into a movie. This is . . . unreal. All of it. Cray-cray.

How will I even begin to tell Belle about this?

Then it gets crazier.

"I have a favour I want to ask of you, Storm," Ivy says. "It's kind of big. I hope you can help me out."

I stare at her. What can I possibly give a musical legend that she doesn't already have? "Uh," I say uncertainly, "sure. If I can help, I will."

Ivy's smile hits me like a pure white lightning bolt.

"I'm so glad you said that. Storm Hall, how would you like to open for me in Honolulu's Aloha stadium on Saturday night?"

26

I am dreaming, of course.

Ivy Baxter isn't really standing in front of me in awesome leather leggings and asking me to sing at her gig. In the same way that bananas don't grow on blueberry bushes, famous pop stars don't wander into family hotel rooms and invite the occupants to sing for them.

I relax a little. Hahaha. Good one. It had me going for a second. The way Ivy is just standing there smiling at me while her bodyguards and her boyfriend make phone calls in the background and help themselves to what's left of the minibar ... as if that would ever happen in real life.

I just need to take a few deep breaths and open my eyes and I will find myself on a pool lounger, where I have clearly fallen into a deep and hypnotic sleep. I hope I put enough suncream on. There's nothing more idiotic than snoozing your way into sunburn.

I sneak my finger and thumb under my opposite arm and pinch myself to prove it.

"YOW!!!"

"Is that a yes?" says Ivy as I leap into the air with a screech while vigorously massaging my armpit.

"You are SO embarrassing," Tina hisses at me through the clenched rictus grin she's directing at Ivy.

"Sorry," I say, my eyes watering with pain. I think I drew blood. "Did . . . did you just ask me to sing at your gig?"

Ivy waggles her beautifully manicured fingers in the air, jazz style. "Spontaneity is the spice of life. Don't you find?"

Spontaneity has its time and its place. That's a quote from something.

"Um," I say.

Ivy sits on Tina's bed. Tina practically chokes

with excitement. If I know my sister – and I do – then she will probably cut the sheet up later and sell it on eBay. (I'm not kidding. She did it with a Coke can she once found near Bruno Mars's dressing room.)

I sit down on my own bed opposite the superstar and order myself to get it together. Oh, and also to breathe. (Don't freak out. DO NOT freak out.)

Ivy's lips are moving. What she's saying is anyone's guess. She could be talking Martian for all the sense I can make of it.

". . . chat through a few song choices though you may have plenty of ideas of your own. Wardrobe is already on alert, we will pick out the cutest outfit you ever saw. Playing with your make-up and hair will be wild – do you do cute or edgy? Maybe edgy. I'll make sure you have a choice. Azaria, my tour manager, will be in touch about security – we will have to ask you sign a confidentiality agreement but don't worry, the whole world is going to know about you when we go public. Lori-Ann will handle the press release. I have a team of PR geniuses who will get your name on every billboard in every country that ever sold one of my records. We'll announce it this afternoon – is that OK with you? If I see one more crazy rumour about a singing dog back-up act, I'll probably detonate."

"I'll get Mum," Tina blurts.

"Do you have an agent, Storm?" Ivy asks as my sister charges out of the apartment.

I stare at the slim brown hands that are suddenly wrapped around my own rather pale ones, and stupidly think of secret agents.

Probably not what she was angling for.

"You should get one." Ivy pulls me to my feet and leads me into the main room, where the bodyguards all put their phones away and smile at me. The Suit offers me a wink. "I know plenty of people who'd fall over themselves to have you on their books. So fresh and young and wonderful! Do you have any ideas about what you'd like to sing? We'd use the tracks from your CD – you have such an exciting sound, did I say that already? – but I think we'll run into licensing issues that I can't be bothered with. Besides, I can't imagine you want to give those idiots any more publicity."

"No," I say. I'm firm about that at least.

Ivy hugs me. "We are going to have so much fun," she laughs into my dusty hair.

Mum and Dad burst into the apartment with Tina behind them.

"IVY!" my dad squeals.

He sounds like he's about ten years old, queuing for autographs at a stage door. I've never seen him so excited. A part of me dies with pure embarrassment.

Ivy looks a little startled at being greeted this way by a fully grown adult male, but she recovers like the pro that she is. "You must be Storm's father. I'm so glad to meet you."

"IVY!" Dad squeals again.

"Forgive my husband," says Mum, shaking Ivy's hand. "He doesn't get out much." (Yeah, and I bet he's hopped up on about six cups of coffee by this time of day.)

"IVY!" Dad has started sobbing. *He's actually sobbing.* (In terms of embarrassing parenting, he just won Father of the Year.)

"Come on, Dad," says Tina, coaxing him towards the balcony. I'm fervently hoping that she will lock him out there. "You need a nice sit-down and an extra-strong coffee for the shock."

To her credit, Mum looks pale but completely composed. "I'm Meggie Hall," she tells Ivy. "Storm's mother and agent. We're not agreeing to anything until I have sat down and read through some kind of contract. Storm is only thirteen years old. If any of this puts her in harm's way, you'll have me to answer to."

Ivy grins at me. "Forget what I said about agents, Storm," she says in amusement. "I think your mother has everything under control."

Mum is now shaking hands with Alec the Suit and the bodyguards. I am so relieved to have an adult in charge that I wonder for a moment if I'm about to burst out crying too.

"Alec?" says Ivy, suddenly brisk and business-like. "Call Frank, get him to send through a contract. And can you get Lori-Ann in here to talk publicity?"

"She's at the stadium."

"Send a car for her. We need to work out a press release that everyone's happy with. We don't have much time."

Alec the Suit is obviously not just Ivy's boyfriend, but part of her management team. I wonder what it must feel like to be bossed around by your girlfriend like that. But Alec doesn't seem to mind. He's already making phone calls as Ivy turns back to Mum.

"Mrs Hall, my PR manager will be here in half an hour to discuss details, does that sound OK?"

"We need to see the contract first," says Mum firmly.

I want to shrivel into the floor. I don't know how Mum can be so bossy with someone as famous as Ivy Baxter.

Amazingly, Ivy smiles. "Of course," she says. "My lawyer is sending it through right now."

Within minutes, a contract has been magically downloaded via Alec's phone. A wireless printer has been produced from somewhere, and paper whirs silently into Mum's waiting hands. I've never seen a contract before. I didn't know they had so many pages.

Mum reads through, scribbling things in the margins with Ivy beside her. Tina is still with Dad on the balcony, though she watches everything through the glass doors with wide eyes. The scribbled-on contract is scanned and emailed back to Ivy's lawyer, and half an hour later a new version appears with all of Mum's changes in place for them to do the same thing all over again. Mum now has a pen in her hand. She seems reassured by what she's reading this time.

How am I feeling? I don't know. My brain is close to overflowing with something: tears, or laughter, or just pure *emotion*. I need some time alone. This is happening so fast . . . I need to think. I can't get under the bed again, so I do the next best thing. I slide out of the room and lock myself in the bathroom.

I sit down on the toilet seat and stare at my hands. Then I pull my phone out of my pocket and ask the world what's going on.

27

Thursday afternoon 4–8 p.m. (Friday 2–6 a.m. in Glasgow)

Ivy Baxter @therealIvyB
Gotta love a rumor. . . #honolulu
↻ 5439 ★ 8863

News 4 Youz @news4youz
Does @therealIvyB have a further surprise in store? Stay chooned! #honolulu #Ivy

Ivy Ivy Ivy @topIvyfangirl
#avaavaava #BFFs4eva

Celebrity News @celebnewsstories

IVY NEWS: Extra act on Saturday night? More
when we have it #Ivy #hawaii

Style_ish @harry4eva

ANY1 ELSE HEARD RUMER 1D SUPORTING
@thereallvyB? #skreeming

HUFFINGTON POST

Ivy Baxter's surprise gig at the Aloha Stadium
in Honolulu on Saturday night looks like it may
have one more trick up its sleeve.

The superstar has already achieved 150 million
record sales and boasts some of the world's
best-selling singles of all time, including "Wipe
Out", "Take Your Pick", "Rainbowz End" and
"Battle Gurl". She has achieved eleven number-
one singles on the *Sensation* Hot 100 chart
and countless music awards, and regularly
features on the Forbes Rich List. But net worth
and musical achievements aside, Ivy is best
known for her love of surprises. And it looks as if

Honolulu – a gig announced just yesterday with a predictable stampede on tickets from as far afield as Russia and Singapore – will be no different. If rumours are to believed, Ivy has lined up a new support act. The superstar is well known for surprising collaborations, performing with artists ranging from international orchestras to high-wire acrobats. Could this secret collaboration be the most surprising of all?

"IT'S THE LARRY LAMORNA SHOOOW...
Hiiii, Hawaii! Social media is in meltdown today following the surprise announcement of an Ivy gig right here in Honolulu. Are you one of the lucky locals who got tickets? What do you make of these latest rumours that Ivy has found a new collaborator for Saturday night? Could it be One Direction? I put the question to our celebrity editor, Pippa. Are the rumours true?"

"It's a possibility, Larry. As our listeners know, One Direction are just across the ocean in China this month with touring dates across the USA

scheduled in the not-too-distant future. Harry Styles's friendship with Ivy is the worst-kept secret in showbiz. If the boys make a detour to our little island, there will be a lot of happy fans out there."

"Thanks, Pippa. The lines are open for you to have your say, Hawaii. Caller on line one, you're live on the Larry Lamorna Show..."

HUFFINGTON POST

Boyband sensation One Direction deny rumours of a collaboration with Ivy Baxter at her Honolulu gig on Saturday. "If I could split myself in half I'd be there," Harry Styles is quoted as saying. "I love Ivy to bits, but Manila have us that night." Fans in the Philippines can rest easy that their evening isn't under threat. So who will share the limelight with the world's favourite diva? With just forty-eight hours to go, fans are discussing acts that range from singing dogs to Finnish cortortionists. It won't be long before Ivy's formidable publicity machine cranks into action, but for now they are staying silent. Ivy herself is clearly enjoying the fun, judging from all the hints in recent tweets.

Wooffles the Wonder Dog @mrwooffles
@therealIvyB happy to discuss terms if interested in collaboration, DM for info

Ivy Baxter @therealIvyB
Not long to go before the big reveal, Hawaii. . .
♥☺
� 5633   ★ 8502

Battle Gurl @Ivy4evaneva
@therealIvyB My fish died pls follow me pls pls pls #Ivy

News 4 Youz @news4youz
IVY COLLABORATION: THE LATEST. 13-year-old wonderkid to open for @therealIvyB in Honolulu. More when we have it

Celebrity News @celebnewsstories

13 years old and about to take the world by

Storm? #Ivy

Wooffles the Wonder Dog @mrwooffles

#woofwoof #Ivy See Wooffles the Wonder Dog

live at the Palace Theatre, tickets still available

Ivy Ivy Ivy @topIvyfangirl

#Storm #Ivy #BBF

Ivy Baxter @therealIvyB

Stormy times ahead? ♥☺#hawaii

🔁 8450 ⭐ 9024

Battle Gurl @Ivy4eveneva

@stormhall_14 My hamsta died pls pls pls follow

me #Ivy

News 4 Youz @news4youz

@stormhall_14 interview? Great terms, DM us #Ivy

Celebrity News @celebnewsstories

#Ivy collaborator revealed as @stormhall_14

more to come

Ivy Ivy Ivy @topIvyfangurl

@stormhall_14 RU 13 or 14? They say UR 13

but UR address is 14 #Ivy4eva

My heart gives a funny lurch to see my actual Twitter handle in these strangers' tweet. But I barely have time to register it before my phone goes completely beserk.

DING-DONG-DING-DONG-DING-DONG-DING-DONG-DING-DONG.

My handle – my name – is *everywhere.*

DING-DONG-DING-DONG-DING-DONG-DING-DONG-DING-DONG-DING-DONG.

I put my phone by the sink, suddenly scared by the way it has burst into life. People are asking me things, selling me things, showing me things. They are pushing themselves out of the screen at me. The bathroom is full of them, crowding around me and yelling at me.

@stormhall_14

@stormhall_14

@stormhall_14

None of the messages are from my friends. It's still the middle of the night in Glasgow. Belle and Colin and Jade and everyone are sleeping while my name is racing around the world.

DING-DONG-DING-DONG-DING-DONG-DING-DONG-DING-DONG—

I reach out my fingers a little fearfully, fumble with the mute button and turn the phone face down. Silence has never sounded so wonderful. Then I gaze at myself in the mirror. My eyes look frightened and way too big for my face.

I don't think I can do this.

28

Someone is knocking at the door.

"Storm? Are you in there?"

I tear my gaze from the mirror, blink a couple of times, and dart a few glances at the phone. It is still face down and silent. I can't imagine what I'll see if I turn it face up again. A hundred messages? A thousand?

"Storm?"

Mum sounds worried. It's an effort but I stand up and unlock the door.

"Everything OK, honey?"

I have probably been in the bathroom for about twenty minutes. I hope she's not going to ask me anything awkward about my digestion.

"Yes," I say. I think I sound normal but I can feel my face crumpling.

It's as if Mum can see right into my heart. "This is a lot to take in, Storm," she says gently, pulling me into a hug. "You're bound to feel a bit shaky."

A *bit* shaky is an understatement. How can I put into words this weird combination of feelings? Elation and terror and sadness and anger and amazement and shock, all of it mushed up together like a big ball of Play-Doh?

"You're doing really well so far," Mum says. "This is your dream. And you've made it happen all by yourself."

I feel a little smile turning up the corners of my mouth. I have, haven't I? Wewehi can jump into the Pacific Ocean with their bongos and their attitude. They aren't *Ivy*.

"But if you're not ready, then you don't have to do this." Mum looks steely for a minute. "I've made sure you can get out of that contract."

My mother really is amazing.

"I can do that?" I ask.

"If you want to." Mum studies my face. "Do you want to?"

Now that I know I can, I don't. All I've ever wanted to do is sing. In the bath, in my bedroom, at the National Choir Finals, supporting Ivy Baxter at the Aloha stadium. . . It's all the same thing. It's singing. *My Thing*.

"No," I whisper. I say it again, more strongly. "No. I don't want to get out of anything."

Mum smiles at me. She understands me so well.

"Um, how many people fit in the Aloha stadium?" I ask, following her out into the apartment.

"About fifty thousand," Mum tells me.

The bathroom is suddenly looking appealing again. But before I can bolt back in there and panic afresh, I realize that the apartment is looking emptier. Ivy and her posse have gone. I can't decide if I feel upset or relieved by this. It's a bit like when you've eaten every bar of chocolate in the house and you know you'd eat some more given the chance, but at the same time you're glad to see a lovely bowl of fresh fruit on the table instead.

Two women are sitting on the sofa, chatting to Dad and Tina about the weather. Who knew pop star people did that? Dad seems to have recovered from his weird screaming fit and is looking reasonably normal again, if you can use that word to describe a fully grown, sunburned coffee addict in an AC/DC T-shirt, cargo shorts and flip-flops.

Mum introduces the women as Azaria, Ivy's tour manager, and Lori-Ann, the publicist.

"I'm so pleased to meet you, Storm." Azaria sounds like she means it.

"I *adore* your jacket," Lori-Ann adds, stroking my faux-fur arm. "We're going to have a riot with your public image if this is your private one."

"I told you packing that jacket was a good idea," says Tina. She grins to let me know that she's joking.

"My public image?"

The publicist nods. Whoa. A public image means CLOTHES. Awesome, eye-catching clothes. Ivy Baxter-type clothes.

I think I'm going to faint.

"Let me take you through what's going to

happen," Azaria says as I sink on to the sofa beside Tina, who takes my hand and squeezes it. "There will be a press conference later today. We will drop teasers about you all over social media. There will be a styling session and photo shoot tomorrow, and interviews and run-throughs and sound checks on Saturday before the gig. How does that sound?"

The shock is finally beginning to wear off because, all of a sudden, I can't stop grinning. I'm going to sing with Ivy Baxter in front of fifty thousand people in just forty-eight hours, and I'm going to smash it. This is everything I have ever dreamed of, and a lot more besides. My horizon is an incredible shade of awesome. The only downer is that it's still too early in the morning back home to talk to Belle about my life-changing few hours.

"My Twitter handle is already out there," I tell Lori-Ann. "Loads of people are asking for interviews and stuff."

"I'll deal with it all," Lori-Ann promises. "In the meantime, if you want to chat with your friends, you might want to do it via a more private channel."

I nod. That makes sense. My stomach has a "crazy spring lamb" moment, leaping and twisting in mid-air for no reason at all. Something tells me it's going to be doing that for a while.

There is a lot to take in, so I do my best to stop watching the clock on the apartment wall to work out when I can call my BF, and instead I listen. Mum is taking notes about call times and private cars and schedules in long loopy writing on the hotel stationery. Dad is making lots of coffee, mainly for him, and Tina is on her phone texting all her friends that her sister is about to become extremely famous. The room clock ticks towards eight p.m. At last I excuse myself from all the planning and hurry to the bathroom.

Seven hundred and thirty tweets. Gulp. I ignore the red-hot "notifications" button and log on to Facebook. Everything on here still looks normal. I can almost believe none of today has happened.

I start writing, my fingers a blur. I am so grateful for WhatsApp because there's no way I could fit this into a hundred and forty characters. The end result is about a hundred lines long and full of weirdly spelled "AAARGH!"s and "WHAAA!"s and "EEEEEK!"s but I get everything in: the recording, the radio disappointment, the Ivy hunt, the under-the-bed disaster, the mega news of Saturday's gig. And then at the end, I ask Belle her news. I'm determined this time not to be a diva and forget that my mates have lives too.

I wanna keep talking about U, famous girl, but thanks 4 asking!! Everyone's got sore throats so we'll probably end up croaking through our song!! #frogchorus Colin's voice is a major surprise tho, really fab

On the subject of Colin I sent him a smiley cat emoji on Twitter the other day do you think he'll think I'm crazy???

You idiot!!

Seriously Belle the smiley cat thing kind
of popped out I don't want him to think I
fancy him or anything

ANYWAY. What were U doing palling up
with Emily and Gwen in that pic?

Photobombing, hehhehehe

Of *course* she photobombed them.

Belle is the photobomb queen. I pull up the
picture again. It's totally clear. Emily and Gwen are
trying to look cool for a selfie and Belle has pogoed
into the side of the picture with a massive grin on
her face and snapped a shot of her own. My BF is a
legend.

29

Friday 2 p.m. (midnight Glasgow)

Bad news first.

I am not a natural at this.

After a restless night full of weird dreams, Mum bangs on our bedroom door at the crack of dawn.

"Time to get up! Exciting day ahead!"

Tina groans and turns over, muttering something about needing another three days' sleep. I sit bolt upright with my heart in my mouth as all the crazy stuff of yesterday floods back into my brain. I'm singing at Ivy Baxter's gig tomorrow night. INSANITY.

"Now would be good," Mum calls again through our bedroom door.

I am already scrambling into the bathroom and reaching for the shower nozzle. No sooner have I turned the water on than I realize my shower gel is on the other side of the bathroom. I step out of the shower, slip on the wet floor and bang my leg on the bathtub. Almost at once, a massive red welt explodes into life on my shin. Just my luck.

I catch a glimpse of myself in the bathroom mirror as I'm muttering and hopping my way back across the room with the shower gel. My hair is soaked and flat on one side, and dry and sticking up on the other. It's not a good look. But that's not what catches my attention. There is a bright red zit between my eyebrows that's almost as big as my shin welt. This is not OK!

"MUUUUM!"

My yell is loud enough to bring Tina zombie-walking into the bathroom, where she cannons off the open shower screen with a scream even louder than mine. Alex and Jake, woken by the chaos, explode through the connecting doors into our room and start bouncing like kangaroos on the beds. Dad shuts himself out on the balcony with his coffee to escape the noise. Mum is the only one close to keeping it together.

"They'll be able to fix it with make-up. Katy Perry and Rihanna both struggle with their skin, but you'd never know it, would you?" (I'm glad she's so calm and reassuring. Honestly, can you imagine if my dad were in charge? Ha!)

"Count yourself lucky you don't have a black eye," Tina moans, one hand clapped over her face. Lori-Ann, the publicist, arrives five minutes later. I've showered but that's as far as I've got. I fix my towel as best I can and put on my most professional smile.

"Constipated, Storm, love?" Dad asks as he comes in from the balcony. "Me too. I think it's the water."

"We only have an hour to get you ready for the press conference, Storm," says Lori-Ann. "It's a pretty tight schedule."

There are three other women with her: one for hair, one for make-up, and one for outfits. Tina peels her hand away from her shower-screen injury to stare at the beautiful things swishing and twinkling on the silver rail that comes into the room behind Lori-Ann's *entourage*. (This is the only word that comes close.)

Oh. My.

"We're only borrowing these, I'm afraid," says Lori-Ann. "So don't get too excited."

That's fine. "Borrow" is my middle name. Only, I usually just get to borrow stuff from Belle and Tina, not hot designer shops. I reach out in wonder to touch a sparkly white dress. My towel – all I'm wearing – chooses this moment to slither off and hit the floor.

Eek. Nudesville.

I do the only thing I can think of. I dive headfirst among the clothes on the rail.

My brothers have spotted the towel and guessed what's happened, if their giggling is anything to go by. Tina and Mum are trying not to laugh, but failing. Dad and the entourage look unfazed. Dad probably hasn't noticed, but clearly for the *entourage*, naked people jumping headfirst into clothes rails is no biggie.

"You're keen," says Lori-Ann.

"You said we're on a tight schedule," I squeak from the depths of a pale purple coat fringed in soft purple feathers. "Can someone pass me my, um. . .?"

Dad and Tina whisk the boys away to breakfast downstairs.

It takes me a while to recover from the embarrassment. I'm still blushing when room-service breakfast is delivered to the door. I am left in peace to have my hair combed and spritzed and teased and pinned and spritzed again between mouthfuls of toast.

"Where is the press conference?" I ask Lori-Ann as the make-up person gets going on my zit. It's going to take a LOT of cover-up.

"Downstairs. It won't take long. We'll handle the questions. All you have to do is look great and smile."

"Storm, how does it feel to be famous?"

Remembering Lori-Ann's advice, I smile. I probably look constipated, like Dad said back in the apartment.

"Storm is delighted," Lori-Ann says. "And so is Ivy."

"How did you meet Ivy, Storm?"

"She gave Ivy a demo CD," Lori-Ann replies.

It feels a bit fangirl-ish when Lori-Ann puts it like that. I want to explain about the Suit but maybe Ivy doesn't want anyone to know about him. This stuff is *hard*. I smile some more.

"What's your favourite band?"

"What designer are you wearing?"

"How long have you been singing, Storm?"

I smile again. I am so paralysed by the banks of cameras and scribbling journalists in this big room in the heart of the hotel that I couldn't speak even if I wanted to.

"Storm has been singing since she could talk," Mum says, sitting next to me and squeezing my hand.

"*Can* she talk?" someone asks at the back, to a burst of laughter.

I should be ready to answer these questions. It's what I've been working for. What I've dreamed of. I can't actually believe what's happening to my body. This is what I've been waiting for and yet my facial movements seem paralysed with total and utter fear. It's like an alien being has literally frozen my face.

"Is she going to release an album?"

I hear the question but there is no reaction – I actually want to hit my own face to wake it up. Please, God, help me NOW!

"Sure, I have so many songs that I'm desperate to share with the world – all in good time," I say in one long breath as if someone punched my stomach.

Finally! I got the words out!

"Thank you for your questions, guys. We'll see you at the stadium tomorrow," says Lori-Ann, efficiently wrapping things up.

There is a volley of camera flashes as the photographers come up close to snap me. I nervously turn my head so my zit is facing the back of the room. I feel a bit like a criminal probably feels when they have a mugshot done, but at least the alien has left my body and I can articulate words again.

"That was great," says Lori-Ann, bustling me out of the hotel towards a waiting car.

"Enjoying yourself?" Mum asks as the car purrs away.

"Mum, you wouldn't believe it – this was my moment, this is the day of my dreams and I froze – it was as if every facial muscle was ignoring my brain. Inside I wanted to cry, scream even, but I couldn't speak."

"Not getting nervous on stage doesn't mean butterflies won't kick in elsewhere, and it seems like they have."

How is it that with one squeeze of my mum's hand I feel as though I am really going to be ok? They are magic those hands, I'm telling you.

"Now, Milady – let's tackle the photo shoot. I know you'll nail it!"

"Where are we going anyway?" Dad asks, peering out of the window.

"Ahh . . . a need-to-know basis," Mum tells him.

"And we—"

"Don't need to know. Ivy's even hotter on security than her reputation suggests."

The car swings down a private road towards a beautiful beach like something out of the movies. Palm trees bend their graceful leaves towards turquoise water and the sand is so white, it's hard to look at.

We pull up beside a glamorous old hotel with a wide deck that faces the beach. I notice that there are lots of people in black dotted around as we are escorted inside. My parents' eyes sweep from left to right like windscreen wipers in heavy rain.

"I've heard of this place," says Dad in excitement, looking up at the big retro façade. "Elvis came here. What a fantastic place for a photo shoot. I wonder what their coffee is like?"

We take a lift straight up to the top floor, where Lori-Ann and the familiar entourage are waiting in a huge, sunlit suite with a massive roof terrace. Luckily I'm not wearing a shower towel this time. It's hard not to gawp at the bustle.

"Storm, welcome to the madhouse."

I whirl around at Ivy's familiar voice. It's hard to resist the urge to grin stupidly as my heroine strides towards me in the most awesome pair of white leather jeans – the only pair of white leather jeans, to be fair – that I've ever seen. Seeing her proves that this is all really happening. The whole press conference thing earlier didn't feel real the way that seeing Ivy does right now.

"Looking good, my little star." Ivy tweaks my cheek as stylists and make-up artists, photographers and runners and bodyguards all mill around us. "Ready to play?"

Mum stays close beside me, trying to act professional but struggling to contain the squeaks of excitement at the gorgeous clothes on the photo shoot rails. The labels make my head spin. They make this morning's dressing-up look like a trip down the high street during the sales.

"So ready," I agree, with not one sign of any alien silence.

Finally, the fun is starting to happen!

30

I've done loads of shots with Ivy now, and I think
I'm getting the hang of it. It felt a bit weird to begin
with, like something Belle and I act out in our
bedrooms. But now I'm flying. Ivy and I (IVY AND
I!!!) have been posing around on this incredible roof
terrace like old-time movie stars. The view up here
is unbelievable: you can see all the way down the
coast, and the sun sparks on the sea like fire on
metal. It's not hard posing in gorgeous clothes in a
place like this. The view and the fabrics make you
want to pull your shoulders back and strut and do
your best Elvis snarl.

"That's lovely!" the photographer cries, sidling

around us like a crab in a black turtleneck and interesting piercings. "Great! Lots of fun!"

I'm messing around with one of the most famous recording artists in the world. Ivy and I laugh and dance and act like we're best mates. It feels like we ARE best mates, actually. Hanging out with her is starting to feel almost normal.

How weird is that?

After about twenty minutes, Ivy pulls off this incredible feather boa thing she's been wearing and tosses it casually at one of the styling assistants before ruffling up her long black hair so that it falls even more perfectly than it fell before. She's SUCH a professional. I make a mental note to practise that exact same move on Belle when we get home.

"Just you by yourself now, Storm. They have all they need of me. I'll see you at the run-through." She is sliding her arms into a jacket that Alec the Suit is holding out for her. "Can't wait!" And she's gone, with just a whisper of her famosity (new word) left on the wind.

"Wow," says Tina, who finally lifts her head out of her phone.

"Wow," I agree. Sometimes, one word is all you need.

The stylists put me in a white trouser suit, then a multicoloured puffball dress, and a sparkly blue jacket covered in studs. Mum starts sunbathing on one of the retro loungers in the background. Tina watches me prancing around in slack-jawed envy. I take pity after a while and ask one of the stylists to let her try on a few outfits too. It feels great to share the fun. Having an older sister in your debt can also be very useful.

After half an hour of pirouetting and posing and reclining in the bright Hawaiian sun, the photographer shows me the screen on the back of his fancy camera. You can't see my zit, even in the close-ups. Magic!

"Can I Instagram some pics of my own?" I ask eagerly, swapping the blue jacket for a strappy maxi dress covered in a delicately beaded skull motif.

Lori-Ann looks up from her phone. "We'll

manage this whole angle for you, Storm. You don't need to worry about a thing."

I'm getting a bit annoyed with Lori-Ann trying to control everything. The world doesn't work like that any more, I want to say. Fashion bloggers snap stuff and put it straight online. No fancy set-up, no contact sheets, no double-checking or confidentiality agreements. My mood starts to dip. I suddenly realize how tired I'm feeling. It feels like I've been on show for HOURS.

"Take a break," suggests the photographer, sensing the sudden atmosphere.

I sit down on a lounger beside Mum with a sigh. A glass of iced water appears beside me, out of nowhere, and I drink it thirstily. Being famous is hard work.

Dad appears, looking anxious. "Has anyone seen the boys?" he asks.

I pause, the water glass still to my lips. Mum sits up. "Aren't they with you?" she says, suddenly alert.

"They were with us when we arrived on set. Then they weren't." Dad passes his hand across his forehead. "The lifeguard says he saw them running into the hotel, but no one can find them."

Mum starts to get up, but I'm quicker. Before Lori-Ann can jump in, I'm kicking my shoes off and hitching up my beaded skull outfit and bolting off the roof terrace. The gown is a bit long on me, and the beads swish around my ankles. It's a nice feeling, if a bit heavy.

"The gown!" squeaks one of the wardrobe girls behind me, but I'm not listening. My brothers are more important.

"Come on," I mutter, pressing buttons in the lift. The doors have barely opened into the reception area before I'm running out of the hotel. Remembering the awesome white retro sunnies the stylist perched on my head ten minutes ago, I yank them down in the glare and take off towards the beach.

I know the boys will be at the beach. I can still see Jake's little face when Dad said they couldn't go there until later. "Two little boys – eight and six – have you seen them?" I ask everyone as I run by.

"They're by themselves, have you seen them?"

I'm getting a lot of funny looks as I run from palm tree to palm tree. My beaded hem leaves a trail in the sand like some kind of exotic lizard's tail. I wonder vaguely how much the dress is worth as I cut across the beach where the sea frills around the edge of the sand, soaking the hem as I run. Probably not as much now as it did when I first put it on.

At last, I spot two little heads busy at the water's edge. My brothers are digging a channel through the sand and watching as the sea fills the hole.

"Jakie! Alex!" I bawl, my hands cupped to my mouth. "Mum and Dad are going to KILL you!"

"Hey, you're the girl in the paper."

I'm only half listening. "Jake! Over here!"

"You are," repeats the voice.

I look round to see two young girls staring at me. One of them has a phone in her hand.

"Uh ... I guess I am," I say. I turn back to my brothers. "JAKE! ALEX!"

Whoosh. A big wave soaks a bit more of my dress. Oops.

255

"Can we take your picture?"

"Sure." I'm waving at my brothers as they charge towards me, kicking up a spray of beachy glitter as they come.

"Storm, catch!" Jake shouts.

He is throwing something right at me. It's hard and flat, with spiky bits on the side. As I reach out to catch it, I realize that it's a crab. The crab nips my hand furiously. I don't blame it. I'd be furious about being used as a frisbee too.

"OW!" I roar.

Another wave soaks me to the knees. I'm too busy shaking off the crab and hugging Jake and Alex to pay much attention. "Please don't run away again," I tell them, squeezing them close. "You're too important."

There are more people gathering around us now, snapping with their phones. I'm so relieved to have found my brothers and that they haven't been eaten by sharks or kidnapped by pirates that I beam and wave and pose, kicking at the water's edge for effect as Jake and Alex dance around my legs. Questions fly around me and I laugh and try to answer them as best I can.

"What's Ivy like?"

"She's a legend!"

"What are you singing tomorrow?"

"Haven't decided yet."

"I wish I was you."

"I wish I was me too," I grin.

"I love your dress!"

"Gorgeous, isn't it? At least," I add with a giggle, "it *was* gorgeous until I took it swimming."

That gets a laugh.

"How do you like Hawaii, Storm?"

I fling my arms up. "I love Hawaii!" I announce. "And I love sand in my toes, and I love sea-watery designer gowns and I love these naughty little guys – they're called Jake and Alex, by the way – and I love EVERYTHING!"

There are paparazzi photographers now among the holiday snappers – guys I recognize from when they were stalking Ivy at our hotel. I give them an extra-big wave. They seem surprised but go with it.

Snap, snap, snap.

"Storm, over here! Give us a smile!"

I pull faces and giggle. Take that, Lori-Ann.

Four guys in black materialize from somewhere. They are holding the growing crowd back, shepherding me and the boys away from the water's edge and up the sand and back into the cool of the hotel, where my soggy, salty gown clings to my ankles and leaves puddles on the white marble floor. Rushing out of the lift with Mum and Dad and Tina, Lori-Ann looks aghast at the damage.

Mum hurls herself at Jake and Alex and hugs them fiercely, shouting at them and kissing them at the same time.

"Oh, my heart... Are you all right, boys? I'm *so cross* with you right now... Jake, you know you should be wearing a hat. The sun at this time of day is so dangerous..."

Lori-Ann is still staring at my dress. I shrug. What does she want me to say? I'm sorry I didn't put your designer gown before my two little brothers? As if.

"Ivy won't like this," Lori-Ann mutters as we all travel back up in the lift. "I need to make a few calls, smooth a few feathers."

"There were photographers everywhere," Jake announces. "And then Storm got bit by my crab."

"It was funny," Alex says.

"I need some coffee," Dad says. "And a very large doughnut."

Lori-Ann still looks pained. I feel a bit sorry for her, but only a bit.

I let the fretting wardrobe girl help me out of my gown and I reach for my phone. There are more notifications than ever. Out of interest, I open Twitter.

I'm trending.

HUFFINGTONPOST

There's a Storm at sea!

Imagine the delight of holidaymakers at the Blue Luau Hotel this afternoon when new teen sensation Storm Hall made an unscheduled appearance on the beach alongside her high-spirited siblings Jake and Alice, wearing a spectacular Versace evening gown beaded in silver skulls (POA).

"I love Hawaii," she told onlookers as she adjusted her Audrey-Hepburn style sunglasses (Chanel, $555) and kicked and splashed around the beach with joyous disregard for a dress more often seen at movie premieres than on the seashore. "I love EVERYTHING!" This is a girl who knows how to grab a headline and make friends in the process: what a combination! Storm will be appearing with Ivy Baxter at Saturday night's greatly anticipated sell-out concert at the Aloha Stadium. If today's performance is anything to go by, we're in for a treat.

31

Saturday 8 a.m. (6 p.m. in Glasgow)

Lori-Ann hasn't said anything, but she's impressed.
I know she is. My ten minutes on the beach have
gone viral in a way that her press conference hasn't.
I think she's annoyed too that she didn't think of
organizing that "unscheduled appearance" for me.
But I guess that's the point of unscheduled stuff –
you can't schedule it.

The US and UK papers are spread around us
in the apartment as we tuck into another room-
service breakfast. There are a few Chinese papers
too, and Spanish, and Urdu, and I don't know how
many other languages. My face is in most of them.

STORM AT SEA! they all shout, or words like that. The pictures are fab. The dress looks even more incredible when I'm twirling and seawater is spraying up in a rainbow arc from all the soggy beads. Jake and Alex – we're still sniggering about the Alice thing – are a bit annoyed that they aren't in any of the pictures, but you can't have everything.

"It's not as if you deserve the attention, boys," Mum says severely, folding up the *Daily Mail* and taking up the *New York Times*. "Running away like that. Try a stunt like that again and I'll microchip you like the cat, see if I don't."

I'm skim-reading the papers and following Twitter and Facebook and Instagram all at the same time. It's multitask mayhem – but fun.

News 4 Youz @news4youz
.@stormhall_14 flavour of the month: sea salt
#stormfever #Ivy #hawaii

Ivy Ivy Ivy @topIvyfangirl
Follow me pls @stormhall_14 U will make my life

"I can't believe how nice everyone's being," I say, scrutinizing a glowing article in the *LA Times*. "There have been a few snarky things on Twitter but that's it."

"They haven't even heard you sing yet," Dad teases.

Mum passes him the *National Enquirer*. STORM HALL: IVY'S SECRET LOVE CHILD?

He spits out his coffee and hides the paper.

I am scrolling through Belle's Facebook feed now. Colin's too, and Jade's, and Bonnie's. Not long until their big show either. Only twenty-four hours until I see them all again.

There's just the small matter of my first-ever stadium gig to get past first.

"Bernie," says Mum suddenly. "What time's our flight tonight?"

"Nine."

"And what time is Storm on stage?"

"Eight," I say.

When the number eight lies on its side, it's the symbol for infinity. I'm going to tattoo the number eight on my wrist as soon as I turn eighteen. I love how it will have one meaning for most people, but two meanings for me.

Mum is sounding alarmed now. "But don't we have to be at the airport two hours before our flight?"

"I'm sure Ivy won't let us miss our plane, Megs," Dad soothes. "I don't know how they work these things, but we'll have priority boarding or something."

"We have to pack," says Mum. Flights always give her the jitters. "We have to be *ready*, Bernie. We can't miss that flight."

"I'm going to join the boys at the pool," says Tina, putting down the papers and standing up.

Ooh. A swim. "I'll come," I say, scattering papers as I stand up.

"Better not, famous girl," says Tina. "Ivy's

sending a car for you in half an hour, isn't she? For your soundcheck and stuff?"

I frown. My sister is right, annoyingly.

"You might have loads of perks," says Tina cheerfully as she picks up her swimming stuff, "but being unfamous has its benefits too. See you later."

"Send Rico my love," I shout after her as the apartment door closes. It's not a great weapon but I use it as best I can. (And who does she think she's kidding? She would LOVE to be in my shoes: literally, since I have some designer sandals left behind from yesterday!)

"Who's Rico?" says Mum beadily.

With my eyes closed, I hold the image of the vast, empty Aloha stadium into my mind. There is an enormous pit at the front of the stage, and the biggest sound desk I've ever seen on this planet, ever, about halfway back. Seats rake up and away on all sides. The lights are hot on my face and there is shouting from the roadies and the steady, echoing sound of scaffolding poles in the wings.

I open my eyes and stare. It's all here. Every last detail. The roadies, the seats, the amps and the wires and the bright arc lights. All that's missing is the crowd. And in just four hours, they'll be here, staring at me and listening to me sing. There might be banners, and balloons, and all the crazy stuff that fans bring to rock gigs. Some of the banners might even have my name on them.

It's just over a week since I stood on the stage at Endrick High, holding Mrs McCulloch's microphone and dreaming of exactly this.

Crazy.

A voice crackles over the tannoy. "Ready, Storm?"

I am so ready. I think I was BORN ready. My palms are a bit sweaty and my heart is running around my ribcage like a maddened rabbit, but that's fine. That's the way it should be.

I lean into the mic.

"Let's go," I say.

For my first song, I've chosen "Make Me a Channel of Your Peace". It's a great song when all's said and done. People think they know it, but, boy. They are in for a surprise. This is my chance to let rip on all the improvs, all the detail that scared Mrs McCulloch back in the Endrick High School hall – and more. With Ivy's amazing band behind me – drums, keyboards, bass, guitar, everything at my disposal – it's going to sound completely awesome. We've run through what I want to do a few times, and these guys are like: "Sure, we can do that," and I totally trust them already because they are professionals who pull all of Ivy's tunes and harmonies from thin air like magicians.

I'm going to name-check Belle and Colin and the National Choir Finals tonight, just before I sing this. There's a symmetry about it which I like. It's the least I can do.

The bass comes in, as deep and bluesy as I could have hoped. Drums crash party rhythms in the background, lead guitar whaling out the tune. Wrapping my hands around the mic, I press my lips to the cold mesh and I sing.

"Make me, yeah, make me a channel pure and true, make me that channel, baby, make it for me and you ... kill the hate, bring the love, feel the wind and stars above, don't despair, I'll be there, bri-i-ng it, oh, bring it if you dare..."

I don't know where the words are coming from, but it feels like they've been there all along, just waiting for the doors to open.

"I do not seek, whoa, I do not seek to hold you, to hold you and enfold you, I just want to love you, to understand you, I'm so-o-o-o-o glad that I found you, make me, oh make me that channel, baby, do..."

There is a distant sound of clapping as the song winds to its wild, joyful conclusion. I open my eyes, feeling a little dazed, to see the guys on the sound desk clapping away. The bass player is nodding at me. Out in the wings, Alec the Suit is smiling at me. Ivy has both her fists in the air.

I think they liked it.

The stadium's conference room is crammed with even more people than we had back at the hotel. I'm still floating on my sound-check cloud and my outfit – a wicked red suit with skinny trousers and sensational platform boots – makes me feel as fierce and strong as Ivy, who is sitting beside me.

"How are you feeling about tonight, Storm?"

"Great," I say. "Couldn't be better. Do you think they do this suit in blue?"

I get a laugh. Lori-Ann nods approvingly in the wings and scribbles something furiously on one of her eternal clipboards.

"How is your protegée standing up to scrutiny, Ivy?" asks a reporter.

Ivy grins. "She's in danger of upstaging me completely."

I blush at the compliment from my heroine. Not even an angel from heaven could upstage Ivy tonight. She looks like a dream in a plunging white trouser suit, her hair in this amazing glossy knot on the top of her head.

"How will you feel when you go back to school on Monday morning, Storm?"

Now *that's* a question. How weird will it be

to find myself back in the Endrick High School corridors, books in my arms and homework on my mind?

"Scared," I say after a moment. "There was this geography exercise I was supposed to hand in last week."

More laughter. I am *loving* this, even though the geography thing is true and kind of worrying.

"Thank you for your time, ladies and gentlemen of the press," says Ivy. "Hope to see you at the gig later."

"Couldn't get tickets!" shouts someone from the back row, which brings the loudest laughter of all.

"You did really well," Alec the Suit tells me as we are ushered off our little dais in a flurry of camera flashes. "You're a natural at this."

Yesterday's assorted disasters are still a little too fresh in my mind for me to entirely agree. Still, it's nice of Alec to say so. And I think maybe I could get good, with a little more practice.

Ivy has done one of her disappearing acts. We

have three hours of kicking around now, before the final round of interviews. Three hours to have lunch, and maybe a nap, and for Mum to coordinate the packing with Dad back at the hotel as best she can. Catching our flight is going to be tight, but Lori-Ann has assured us that it'll all work fine. Then it's hair, make-up, final sound checks – and away.

Bring. It. ON.

Lori-Ann and her minions escort me and Mum to my dressing room, up on a floor near the top of the stadium.

I have a dressing room. Yay!

It's small, but it has a big window that looks over Honolulu, and there's a lovely bunch of flowers on the table from Ivy. I take the card and stare at it.

Sing like you did at the soundcheck and you'll do great.
Ivy xx

I take a photo and Instagram it.

Believe me, you would too.

I do a swift calculation in my brain and – OK – on my fingers too.

EEP.

Have I missed the chance to wish Belle good luck for her show?

Being ten hours behind everything at home is a NIGHTMARE.

I grab my phone with my heart in my mouth. I text Colin too. It's a tough one to compose at speed because I can't sound like I fancy him AT ALL.

After several minutes of indecision, I go for a simple, "Good luck, Colin." Can't really go wrong with that.

32

You must be going nuts!!!

Not nervous actually. Hungry tho. Got 2
your venue OK? xx

Journey was boring despite Colin's jokes. U
looked great in that bead dress xxx

That was SOOOO funny, but I could
have killed Jake and Alex!!!

Don't kill them. Employ them. Media loves little kids.

Media can have them!!!

We giggle about stupid stuff for a bit. Although it's only texts, I can hear Belle's voice in my mind. I hear about Jade's latest crush, on a guy in Year Eleven whose girlfriend is maybe the scariest person in the entire school. I can see that going SO wrong. Bonnie had a party on Wednesday where Sanjit broke his leg. (It must have been some party.) Colin's trousers are still too short.

Do U fancy Colin, Storm?

No WAY it's like fancying a pet!!

I like our pet!

U know what I mean

Just checking.

Gotta go. Being called to stage!

AAAARGH! GOOD LUCK STORM!

xxxxx

I hope Belle and Colin will be OK. I hope they enjoy their moment in the spotlight as much as I'm enjoying mine. I hope lots of things.

"Mum," I say. "Can we get home radio here?"

Mum is in the middle of firing texts at Dad about packing the bags and checking out and printing boarding cards and not losing the boys. She's in that mode now. "Don't know, love," she says without looking up.

I need a connection to the internet. I decide to head up to the roof and try my luck there.

There are stairs outside my dressing room that head in a roofish direction, so I go that way. A few bars of internet waver on my screen as I climb. Taking the stairs two at a time, I tap in the radio address.

"*Kshssh. . . Whksshhh. . .* Choir Finals coming live from Londo— *krrrsshhhh. . .*"

Up another flight, the phone to my ear.

"*Khhrrshhh*. . . first to perform are Endri—*ksshgshh*. . . ."

That's it! Right there! Man, this is annoying. Belle and Colin will be on at any minute and all I can hear is the crinkling of a thousand crisp packets.

Right at the top of the stairs, the reception clears.

Belle is singing.

"Make me a channel of your peace, where there is hatred let me bring your love. . ."

I am frozen to the spot, clinging to my phone, willing her on. She's note perfect.

Colin next.

"Where there is injury, your pardon, Lord, and whe-e-ere there's doubt, true faith in yo-ou-you. . ."

Nice bit of improv, Colin, I think. Who'd have thought he had it in him?

The rest of the choir comes in with a great swoosh for the chorus. It's so weird to think that I'm on a Hawaiian stadium roof, listening to my mates all those thousands of miles away. . .

They're sounding wonderful but the reception is crackling again.

"Where there is darkness *ksshhwrrrr*— light, and where there's *whshshsh* joy. . ."

GRRRR!

"*Kksshsh whssish WHEEEEEE sksshr*—" Applause.

I shake the phone furiously, waggle it from side to side. Applause turns to a snowstorm, then back to applause again with a bit of talking.

Belle and Colin will have to tell me the result when I get back home tomorrow. I stow the phone in my pocket before taking a moment to gaze at the Honolulu skyline. It's pretty awesome. Silver buildings shooting into the bright blue evening sky. The sea curling away at the shore. The sound of wind and car horns and sirens.

And somewhere down there, fifty thousand people waiting to hear me sing.

You know how Mum's been panicking about missing our flight?

I think we're going to miss our flight.

We're running late.

The buzz from the crowd in the stadium is growing louder. Everyone is running around talking into headpieces. You could cut the air with a knife. A spoon, even. Something really blunt anyway.

My nerves are kicking in, BIG time. My teeth are chattering, and I'm boiling hot as people fuss around me with powder puffs and enough hairspray to stop a woolly mammoth in its tracks.

I press my fingers hard into the arms of my chair as a stylist shows me two choices of jacket: one shocking pink, one canary yellow. I can't choose. I can hardly speak.

I'm not nervous about performing, by the way.

I'm nervous about NOT performing.

Any minute now, Mum is going to say that I can't do this. That I have to jump in a taxi with her right now, hairspray and all, and leg it to the airport. This whole thing has been a mistake, a mistake, a mistake...

"Storm Hall to the wings, please. This is your five-minute call."

278

The sounds from the stadium are growing louder all the time. Someone has put the pink jacket on me. I'm glad because it was the one I liked best. Maybe I communicated that somehow with my eyebrows? I certainly didn't use my mouth. These guys must be good at second-guessing nerve-crazed performers.

"Four minutes," says the tannoy.

Someone applies a final slash of pink lipstick to my lips, a sweep of glittery powder to my cheeks. Alec the Suit appears like a mirage, escorting me towards the stage, telling me to mind the cables and lights and banks of computer screens. People are all wishing me well, patting me on my bright pink shoulder, chucking me under the chin.

"Go for it."

"Enjoy yourself out there."

"Three..." says the tannoy.

Here in the wings, you can really hear the screaming. It's like my dream, only so, SO much more. I clench my fists to my sides and close my eyes.

"STORM! STORM! STORM!"

My name. *They are yelling my name.*

"Two. . ."

Remember to breathe. Remember, remember, remember. Don't pull me away, Mum. Whatever you do, don't pull me away from this.

"One. . ."

There is a massive drum riff. My cue.

I have a cue.

"Break a leg," Alec the Suit says as I run for the stage.

I glimpse an enormous figure with massive hair and a bright pink jacket on a vast screen. I wave. She does too.

It's me.

"Hello, HAWAII!!!!" I shout into my microphone.

The roar engulfs me. I am a surfer riding a wave. I am a skydiver plunging through the clouds.

"STORM! STORM! STORM!"

Thrum goes the bass. *Wham* go the drums. *Tcha* goes the guitar. Up go my fists.

My life starts right here, right now.

I hear my cue.

I lift my first leg forward to begin my ascend on to the stage. I can feel my arm tremble as I bring the mic up to my mouth.

This is it.

I give myself a little shake to pull myself together. This is what I live for, this is the dream. I look down to the audience where I see Dad and Mum grinning at me, attempting to placate my innermost fears. Somehow it all feels right. Like I was destined for this moment. I open my mouth and belt out my first wobbly note.

I am in.

My nerves calm down and I begin to move around the stage. I can hardly take the grin off my face as I dance and slide and jump around. The adrenaline is everything. I know that this is what I want to do for the rest of my life.

My life, condensed into ten glorious minutes.

The crowd love me, and I love them back.

I want to do it all over again.

I want to stay on this stage for ever, waving and dancing and singing. But I can't. It's Ivy's turn to sing, and it's my turn to leave. The pink jacket is removed. Ivy is hugging me, and spinning away on to the stage to do what she does best in the whole world. The Suit is shaking my hand. Numbers and kisses are exchanged. Everything is going by so fast, I hardly dare blink or I will miss it.

Mum is a gibbering wreck. "I can't believe we've left it so late!" she squeals, practically throwing me in the back of the big black Jeep which has just pulled up. Tina and the boys are already in the car. "I'm going to be sick, Bernie. They'll have closed the gates. . ."

"It's OK, love," says Dad, nursing an extra-large cardboard cup of his beloved beverage of choice. "The flight's delayed."

Mum sags against the luxurious leather seats like an old cushion. "Oh, thank heavens," she says weakly.

"Stop picking your nose, Jake," Dad advises as the driver speeds around Honolulu towards the airport. "You've already had one nosebleed today."

"Two nosebleeds now," Alex pipes up helpfully,

bouncing on the Jeep's big leather seats.

Mum is back to her more focused self as she fishes around in her bag for tissues to stem the flow from Jake's nose. Tina furiously applies more make-up, chewing her lip. I guess she's thinking about what might have been. Dad dandles Alex on his knee and slops coffee on the Jeep's leather seats.

"Isn't anyone going to ask how I got on?" I say hopefully.

"Nope," Tina growls, snapping shut her make-up mirror.

And that, folks, is life in this family.

33

Saturday 8 p.m. (Sunday 6 a.m. Glasgow)

Even though our flight has been delayed, we still have a mad whirlwind dash at the airport.

"Hurry," Mum screeches at us, slaloming her luggage trolley through the crowd like an Olympic skier. "We've been lucky so far, but the gate will close at any minute..."

Alex and Jake sail along on Dad's luggage trolley, their hair flying in the breeze and their shorts flapping around their little brown legs. They've had a good holiday, I think, even though they didn't get to do *everything* they wanted.

I slip my hand silently into Tina's, dragging her in Mum and Dad's wake, and wonder briefly if I will be chased aboard the plane by photographers or something exciting like that. I glance around, but can't see any cameras.

"I can't believe I missed the gig for Rico," Tina groans.

"There'll be other chances," I tell her, but I don't think she believes me.

It makes me wonder if I'll ever do anything like this in my life again.

(Whoa, stop that depressing thought RIGHT THERE. This is only the beginning.)

I look around again for photographers. They are being very slow. I guess we did leave the stadium like rockets.

"Faster," chides Mum. "Faster!"

I wipe my forehead, which is getting sweaty. I haven't had a minute to come down from my adrenaline high yet. Running through the airport like a nutter doesn't quite tally with what was I doing only half an hour ago.

We check in our bags, Jake has a wee, we check in a bag we forgot about, Alex has a wee, we shuffle through security, Jake and Alex both have a wee – "Really, Bernie, how much have the boys had to drink today?" – we leg it down the travelator towards our gate and we squeal into the departure lounge for flight number BA4992.

Tina collapses on a bench, heaving for breath. I collapse beside her. I bet Ivy doesn't have stress like this when SHE travels. I bet she just gets Alec the Suit to call up the airport to fix a nice quiet private jet for her to catch in her own good time, with a red carpet across the runway and chocolate ice cream in her own personal fridge.

I vow to myself that I will travel that way one day.

Our flight is practically empty. It's clear to me that every single person in Honolulu is still at Ivy's gig.

I am feeling twitchy and weird. There are still no photographers.

I take out my phone.

Already, my evening is taking on the quality of a dream. I feel anxious. What if I forget what the whole experience felt like? What if I forget the whole experience, full stop?

"So what was it like?" asks Tina as we lean breathlessly against the long plate-glass windows of the departure lounge after a particularly vigorous game of musical departure lounge chairs that Jake and Alex and Dad are still playing. Mum is sitting at the far end of the lounge, pretending she doesn't know us.

"What was what like?" I say.

"The gig, duh."

I smile. "It was cool."

"Don't tell me that."

"Fine," I shrug. "It was awful. Terrible. Worst evening of my life."

Tina nudges me with her elbow and an irresistible grin.

"Tina," I say.

"Mm?"

"It did happen, didn't it?" I want to check because

I'm losing my grip on everything right now. "Do you think everything will be different when we get home?" The thought scares me a bit.

"Probably," Tina says. "But don't think you're getting the window seat the whole way home just because you're famous now."

Tina is, unfortunately, right. We didn't even get an upgrade on the flight, the assistant just smiled at me, firmly blocking the way to first class.

The rest of the flight is smooth. I don't get any sleep. I just stare over Tina's shoulder at the stars outside the little window. There's no Wi-Fi on this flight, so I don't know what's going on in the world. Did Belle and Colin smash it? Did Endrick High School win the competition?

I guess I'll find out tomorrow.

Every now and then I get my phone out, to scroll through the photos I took. I didn't take many, surprisingly. Too many people taking pictures of *me*, I guess.

One picture shows me and Ivy in the wings

of the stadium just after the soundcheck. I have been singing along to every single word of every single song that Ivy does, even the new ones she's promoting for her most recent album. Ivy stands with me like a goddess. There's a glow around her from the arc lights on the stage. At least, I think it's the arc lights. Maybe it's just her total famosity. (Yeah, I'm liking that word.)

She has her arm around me, and she's pulling a face at the camera. Mum took it. I can tell because it's a bit wonky and not as much in focus as I'd like it to be.

I stare at the picture for a long time. I'm sorry I didn't hear the gig for real, but I got the dress rehearsal and a lot more besides. Ivy Baxter's number in my phone. Ivy Baxter's flower message in my pocket. Ivy and me, me and Ivy.

Who needs sleep?

34

"What time is it in New York?"

Tina is asleep, her head lolling against the window. There is an attractive bit of drool escaping from her mouth. I prod her again.

"Tina, what time is it in New York?"

"Dunno," she says, peeling open a baleful eye. "Bedtime?"

"We're landing in twenty minutes," I tell her. "But I'm so confused about the time zones that I don't know if I can call Belle from the airport. They're in London all day today and back home tomorrow morning. What if it's three o'clock in the morning or something?"

"Don't call her then," Tina yawns.

I've had ten hours in a plane with no sleep and I'm jumpy and I want to talk to my BF. I have had so much time to THINK about stuff that I feel I might explode if I can't communicate with Belle. As we descend, I annoy Tina with pointless questions and random New York facts like that one about Einstein's eyeballs that Colin tweeted me last week. She's very relieved when we land at JFK and she can turn on her phone and lose herself in social media for a bit.

I turn on mine too. Check my Twitter feed: still mental. Check a few pics – don't know if I'll ever get used to seeing myself splashed around Google like this.

"How much would it be for me to call Belle's mobile?" I ask Mum.

"Most of your pocket money into next year," Mum replies in her warning voice.

"Seven hour stop-over in New York," says Dad

brightly as we shuffle down the plane aisle towards the exit. "Who wants to get a taxi into the city for some sightseeing?"

"Can we go up the Empire Tate Building?" Jake asks.

"Empire *State* Building," Dad corrects. "No. But we can drive past it."

"Can we go to the Statue of Liberty?" Jake asks next.

"You have to get a boat, Jake, and we won't have time."

"Can we go to Santa's Grotto? Can we go to Disneyland?"

Dad looks confused. "This isn't Florida, Jake, and it's not Christmas."

"Will the taxi be red?" Alex asks.

"Taxis are yellow in New York, Alex."

Alex looks unimpressed. "I like red taxis."

My brothers have both lost interest now. Dad looks hopefully at me and Tina.

"When you say sightseeing, Dad," I say, "you mean literally *seeing the sights* for five seconds through the taxi window, and then driving back to the airport?"

Dad doesn't seem to think there's anything weird in this suggestion.

"Via New York's best coffee shop, of course," he says, waggling his eyebrows in what he thinks is a tempting fashion.

"I don't think you're selling it to them, Bernie," says Mum. "Anyway, I don't think we'll have time."

Her phone is flashing with about fifty messages, most of them starting with: STORM HALL. I have a funny feeling the craziness is about to happen all over again.

"Ivy's New York agent is waiting for us in the airport," Mum explains. "Half the New York press want an interview. She's supposed to be at the gate when we get off. . ."

But there's no one waiting for us at our gate with a big flashing "Storm Hall this way" sign above their heads.

"They'll find us if they want us," Mum declares

after we've hung around for a while. "We have baggage to collect. Come on."

Changing airports is a pain. We have to fetch our bags, get them right across the city (Dad will get a bit of "sightseeing" in after all), then check them in all over again. One day, I decide, I'll have people who will call people who will fetch my old suitcase with the ragged corners and lug it into taxis for me. Until then, I have to suck it up.

The first thing I see in baggage reclaim is a massive jumbotron with my face all over it. I freeze in my tracks. It's ultra weird, seeing my face in a place I've never been too before. Especially blown up monster big.

A STAR IS BORN! says the scrolling headline under my face. TEEN SENSATION DUE IN NEW YORK THIS MORNING.

"Storm's on TV," says Alex, pointing.

A couple of people turn. Recognition is instant.

"You're Storm Hall!"

"You sang with Ivy in Hawaii last night, right?"

"Look, Marnie, it's the kid from the screen!"

Mum, Dad, Tina and the boys disappear in the sudden press around me. I smile and wave for their cameras as best I can. To be honest, I'm a bit freaked out. After my peaceful flight from Hawaii, I'm not prepared for this.

"What's Ivy like, Storm?"

"How was your flight?"

"Do you like New York?"

I wonder how I'm supposed to answer that last question when I've only been in New York for about ten minutes. "Um—"

"I love your outfit – where is it from?"

I look down at my jeans and T-shirt. It's hardly the most glamorous outfit I've worn in the last few days.

"My sister," I say honestly.

"Storm!"

"Over here, Storm!"

"Give us a wave!"

I have to say, I'm quite relieved when a very tall lady with short black hair and a spotless white suit carves through the crowd like an ice-breaking ship across the frozen Arctic to rescue me.

"Hi, Storm, I'm Tekla, Ivy's representative on the East Coast," she says, shepherding me through the crowd with Mum and the others. "I'm so sorry, we were supposed to meet you straight from the gate but the delay to your flight caused havoc with our communications. Now, Ivy left strict instructions that you and your family were to be looked after, so if you could follow me, we'll find you some food and do a little make-up and styling before your interviews, OK?"

"What about our bags?" Mum asks beadily.

"We have people on that for you. Everything will be transferred in time for your flight from La Guardia this evening. We've arranged for a limo to get you to the airport later."

"Limo," says Alex in wonder.

I feel myself relaxing into the equivalent of a big, hot bath. *Now* we're talking.

Tekla ushers us through a big glass door into a spacious VIP lounge. The door closes on the noise outside with an expensive thump, reducing the sound to precisely zero. I try not to look TOO much like a gawping country bumpkin and more like the kind of person who gets into VIP lounges most days. Jake and Alex are so overawed that they are actually behaving themselves for once, clinging on to Mum and Dad's hands and goggling through the vast plate-glass windows at the taxiing jets. Alex will be abandoning his universal love of cars for planes at this rate.

"Make yourselves comfortable," Tekla says as we go through *another* glass door into an even *more* VIP bit of the VIP lounge. "They'll take your orders for lunch in a moment. Stylists, make-up and wardrobe will be with us in forty-five minutes."

"This place is brilliant," Tina breathes.

The walls are painted Dad's favourite colour (coffee) and there are big marble pillars and low glass tables and lots and lots of plants and cool black-and-white photos on the walls. Waiters buzz around us, taking orders for anything we want. The boys order burgers; Dad asks for coffee and a club sandwich because he thinks it sounds cool and

New-Yorkish; Mum has soup because she's worried about the cost.

"Mum, Tekla said all this was COMPLIMENTARY," I say as her soup arrives with a roll and one pat of butter.

"My club sandwich hasn't complimented me yet," Dad says. "And I thought I was looking pretty good."

"Complimentary means free, Dad," I tell him patiently, but he's laughing too loudly into his coffee to reply. (See? Again with the Dad jokes. You can't take him anywhere.)

Mum is determined to be cautious. "There's no such thing as a free lunch, Storm. Haven't you heard that expression? Have you seen the prices on this menu?"

Tina goes for a salmon sandwich. I have pastrami on rye, because I've always wanted to do that in New York and I have totally no idea what pastrami OR rye are. (Turns out that pastrami is a salty kind of beef and rye is this special bread. Who knew?)

Lunch over, I take a luxurious shower in the

executive shower room and use every single complimentary product lining the shower-room shelf. When I come out, stylists and make-up and wardrobe have set out their now-familiar wares in a corner of our VIP room. I have six interviews to do before our limo (YES – you read that right – LIMO!) takes us across the city to La Guardia.

This whole fame thing is one crazy circus.

35

(Sunday. Time has lost ALL meaning)

Wow, I'm tired. I've answered about a million questions, all about the same thing. My clothes, Ivy, my school, Ivy, my future, Ivy. It was fun for the first half an hour. Then it got boring. But I know that professionals *have to maintain enthusiasm at all times* so I kept smiling and saying the same thing over and over. Yes, Ivy heard my CD. Yes, the dress on the beach was very expensive. Yes, the gig was amazing, extraordinary, LIFE-changing. But please can I go home now?

I didn't say that last bit. I was just thinking it for

the last hour and a half. Now we only have two hours until our flight home. A proper conversation with my best friend is within touching distance. Well, within the total distance of the Atlantic Ocean anyway.

"Limo," says Alex dreamily.

It's all he's said since the limo – a real, honest-to-goodness limo with a bar and lights down the middle of the carpet and three roof windows and EVERYTHING – pulled up at JFK and we were bundled into it with a few final waves at the crowd and a million selfies with my sister and all my new-found American friends. I stroke my bright pink jacket lovingly and lean my head against Mum's with a sigh of contentment.

Right at the end of the last interview, Tekla handed the jacket to me with a smile. I gaped. I could have sworn it had been whipped off my back moments after leaving the stage at the Aloha stadium.

"Ivy sent it over from Hawaii for you," Tekla explained, seeing the expression on my face. "She knows it was your favourite."

La Guardia is about twelve miles from JFK. The road purrs away beneath the limo's wheels like a cat, the ride as smooth as skating on ice, in between the traffic jams and the traffic lights that dog the way.

"Limo," Alex groans again.

"Do you have our tickets, Bernie?" says Mum as we pull up at Departures. "Do you have our passports?"

"Nope," says Dad.

Mum almost detonates with terror until she remembers she stowed our tickets and passports in one of the million side pockets on her handbag.

Tekla is waiting as we climb out of the limo. How on earth did she get here so quickly? She either has a helicopter or a very fast horse.

"I have arranged a private room at your gate. You could use a little privacy after those interviews, I'm sure."

This room has even more complimentary pastries than the one at JFK.

"You'll have to get famous more often, Storm," Tina says.

She smiles flirtatiously with the dark-eyed waiter hovering around Mum. "Are you sure this glass of champagne is free?" Mum is saying.

"I'll do my best," I say, happily attacking a large cinnamon bun.

It gets better. When it comes to boarding, we go on first. As we walk down the concertina tunnel and set foot on the pale blue carpet of our plane, the air stewardess smiles and holds her hand – to the left.

"This way, please, Miss Hall. Miss Baxter made reservations for you all in First Class today."

"Oh, Bernie," says Mum faintly as we walk into First Class. "There are even bar stools."

"Show me the coffee menu," says Dad, rubbing his hands.

Tina puts her arm round my shoulder and squeezes me wordlessly. This is big love from my sister.

"You've done well, sis," she says, when she can speak.

Alex is staring at the set of toy cars which have been laid out for him in our corner of First Class. "Are they for me?" he says.

"You can lie down in a full-length bed," Mum says in ecstasy. "Oh, Bernie, I'm never travelling Economy again."

"I was afraid of that," says Dad.

I bet Ivy travels first class all the time, I think, as I gaze around the elegant cabin. I can't imagine having this much luxury in my life all the time.

Actually, scrap that. I can. I can imagine it all too well.

I settle down in my huge comfy seat with my huge personal TV screen and more buttons down the arm of my chair than the pilot probably has in the cockpit. If I've learned anything from those ten fabulous minutes on stage at the Aloha Stadium, it's that you have to enjoy every second of times like these, because the good stuff has a habit of passing you by like a flash of lightning.

Every...

Single...

*

"Twenty minutes until we land, Storm," says Mum, rubbing my shoulder. "You've slept the whole way!"

I stretch and blink up at the cabin lights. Then I sit up very fast indeed.

"We're here?" I say, aghast. "Already?"

We can't be. I had PLANS. I was going to watch movies, and eat amazing food, and maybe even get a shoulder massage!

"I would have woken you earlier for a shower," says Mum, "but you looked so peaceful lying there, it was a shame to wake you up. You've had a tough couple of days."

I could have had a *shower*?

"Great breakfast," Dad adds. "I saved you a croissant. Jake ate the rest."

He waves a cold croissant at me, scattering crumbs across a nearby sheikh.

"Don't tell me any more about what I've missed," I groan, clasping my head in my hands. My hair feels weird. I've slept on it, so it's totally flat at the side.

I take the croissant glumly. The best the

stewardess can offer me at this late stage is a glass of freshly squeezed orange juice, which I accept with bad grace. There's just time to go to the most spacious airline loo I've ever seen, wash my face and hands and. . .

I look at myself in the mirror, appalled. There's a massive, scar-like pillow crease mark on my cheek. I look like I've run through a glass window or something. I can see the headlines now: TEEN SINGER: SURGERY HORROR!!!

"I wonder if the paps will be waiting for you at the airport, Storm?" says Tina as the plane banks, preparing to descend. She grins. "They're going to love your 'fresh as a daisy' airline look."

"Shut up," I moan. I pat and press my cheek and hair, hoping to bring the crease marks and flatness under control. I know it's not working.

"Would my baseball cap help?" Mum suggests.

I pull Mum's cap down over my hair. It's a really bad one with a Hawaiian palm tree on the front, but it's better than nothing.

"What am I going to do about my face?"

"Nothing you can do about your face," says Tina. "You were born with it. Unfortunate, but that's life." (She's spending too much time listening to Dad's tragic jokes – they're rubbing off.)

"Perhaps you can walk through the airport with the left side of your face towards a wall at all times," Dad suggests.

It's one thing being photographed when you've had a whole team of stylists sorting you out beforehand. It's something else when you have to go it alone after a ten-hour flight and your face looks like a pile of used wrapping paper on Boxing Day.

"Ah, home sweet home," says Tina while I'm panicking. She leans her head against the window and stares out at the grey early morning light. "Look, you can see the Clyde!"

"That's not the Clyde," says Dad. "That's the Thames."

Tina looks shocked. "Since when did the Thames flow into Glasgow?"

"Since your mother booked our return flights to

London as it was three hundred pounds cheaper," says Mum briskly. "We'll take a coach from Victoria back to Scotland."

Tina groans so loudly that the crumb-covered sheikh looks alarmed.

"Muuum! It'll take us *hours* to get home..."

"What are a few more hours in the name of budget, Valentina?"

Tina lapses into a sulk, which lasts until the wheels of our Airbus touch down on the tarmac of London Heathrow. The creases on my face aren't going down, no matter how much make-up I put on them. I can't go through the airport looking like this. I'll end up in every tabloid in the country looking like I've gone ten rounds with Paddy McPillow, laundry terror of the skies. *What am I going to do?*

Wait.

"We're in London?"

I've had an idea. As the seat belt signs go off and all the rich First Class people around me languidly stand up and smooth down their expensive, totally uncreased clothes and pull down even more expensive handbags and shopping bags from the overhead lockers, I switch on my phone.

Belle, U in London?

Just leaving the hotel. You?

"What are you typing there, Storm, your new novel?" says Dad as my fingers zoom across my phone in a blur of Pacific-blue nail polish.

"Trust me, Dad," I say. "And do exactly what I say."

The noise as we approach the Arrivals hall is intense. I don't think I'm imagining the sound of clicking cameras, or the voices shouting my name. If my face was on a big screen in New York, you can bet your bottom dollar it's on a screen here too.

My plan *has* to work.

The whole way down this long corridor from baggage reclaim, I've kept my face to the wall like

Dad suggested, and Mum's Hawaiian cap down over my eyes, and it's been OK so far. But the tricky bit is coming up.

"There's loads of cameras, Storm," says Tina, peeping round the corner to the Arrivals hall. "Urgh, loads of people are waving your picture around. Have they got no taste?"

Part of me really wants to see what Tina's describing. Remembering my facial disaster zone, the rest of me is happy to let it slide. I take off the baseball cap in case the word is out that I'm wearing one (TEEN SENSATION IN FASHION DISASTER HAT!), and pull my hair into a tight bun on the back of my head with a scrunchie. I flip up the hood on Dad's (way too big and ugly) hoodie and settle my sunnies back on my nose. It's the best I can do.

"The door you want is that way, Storm," says Dad, pointing furtively over my shoulder to the side of the teeming Arrivals hall. "All we have to do is get past the fuzz. I mean, the photographers."

"You're enjoying this way too much, Bernie," says Mum.

I look at Tina. She nods back. We're ready.

"Cue . . . Alex," I say.

Alex starts screaming exactly as planned.

"MUM!" he yells, walking into the Arrivals hall. "I've lost my MUM!"

"Good luck, my loves," says Mum. "See you round the side in a bit."

Then she goes rushing off too, her eye firmly on Alex the whole time, shouting, "HAS ANYONE SEEN MY LITTLE BOY?"

"MUM!" shouts Alex, grinning.

"BABY!" Mum shouts back, scooping him up and covering him with kisses.

Everyone in the hall has stopped avidly watching the doors for me and is staring at Mum and Alex's touching reunion. *Gotcha!*

"Why did Alex get to do that bit?" Jake complains as Tina, Dad, he and I rush our trolley through the hall, away from Mum and Alex, with our heads down and our eyes firmly fixed on a small side door that nobody but us is looking at. "I'm much better at screaming. Where are we going? Why aren't we going with Mum and Alex?"

Dad has reached the door already and is pushing it open.

Success.

We run out into the bright morning light. The bus is there, right where Mrs McCulloch said it would be, idling on the kerb. Thirty faces are pressed up against the glass as Dad, Tina, Jake and I charge towards the open doors. I can hear people shouting my name, but they're people I know and people I like and people I trust and people who won't care about pillow creases on my face or bad hoodies.

"Storm! STORM!!!"

Dad lifts Jake into the bus and shakes hands with Mrs McCulloch. Tina grabs a seat and puts on her headphones and acts like she's totally above all the drama and is only riding this coach as a favour to everyone aboard.

"STORM!!" Jade Miller is the first one to reach me, pulling me into a hug. "YOU'RE SO TOTALLY FAMOUS! OMG I WISH I WAS FAMOUS TOO!"

I extricate myself from Jade, grin at Sanjit, and Bonnie, and Daniel McCready, and all the people shouting and yelling and cheering my name.

"STORM!"

Belle is pushing through the crowd, her eyes glowing. It looks like she's holding hands with Colin but I think it's just the angle.

"Hey, superstar-diva-face-in-all-the-papers-name-on-TV best mate," she says.

"Did you win?" I ask.

"We came second." She shrugged. "Not bad."

"I heard you on the radio," I say, and I hug her. "You sounded awesome."

Belle goes pink with pleasure. "You think?"

"I totally do," I assure her. "You were exactly the right person for that solo." And I mean every word.

"Your first-class seat awaits," Belle says. "It's the best seat we could get you at short notice."

"Sorry it's by the loos," Colin adds beside her. "No one else wanted it."

They *are* holding hands.

Belle and Colin are holding hands.

I don't have time to process what this means or how I feel about it before Mum comes jogging along the pavement towards the bus, pushing the luggage trolley with one hand and propelling Alex along with the other.

The bus pulls away without a single photographer giving chase.

I glance back at Belle and Colin's joined hands.

Everything's perfect.

I think.